Kam came toward her and took her hand, leading her onto the flat rock, then exerting gentle pressure as he said, "Sit."

Jen sat, as much to escape the touch of his hand as from obedience. Memories of the kiss fluttered uneasily in her body.

"Now, breathe the cooling night air and watch the sunset," Kam ordered.

I don't want the beauty of the desert creeping in, she wanted to say. *It is too seductive, too all-encompassing.*

But his was the name that trembled on her lips as he lifted his head, the better to see her face in the dusk light; his the name she whispered as she leaned into him and raised her mouth to his again.

MEREDITH WEBBER says of herself, "Some ten years ago, I read an article which suggested that Harlequin was looking for new medical authors. I had one of those 'I can do that' moments, and gave it a try. What began as a challenge has become an obsession, though I do temper the 'butt on seat' career of writing with dirty but healthy outdoor pursuits, such as fossicking through the Australian Outback in search of gold or opals. Having had some success in all of these endeavors, I now consider I've found the perfect lifestyle."

CLAIMED BY THE DESERT PRINCE
MEREDITH WEBBER

~ POSH DOCS ~

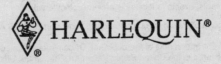

HARLEQUIN®

TORONTO • NEW YORK • LONDON
AMSTERDAM • PARIS • SYDNEY • HAMBURG
STOCKHOLM • ATHENS • TOKYO • MILAN • MADRID
PRAGUE • WARSAW • BUDAPEST • AUCKLAND

PLEASE RECYCLE
THIS PRODUCT IS RECYCLABLE

Recycling programs
for this product may
not exist in your area.

ISBN-13: 978-0-373-52718-2
ISBN-10: 0-373-52718-7

CLAIMED BY THE DESERT PRINCE

First North American Publication 2009.

Previously published in the U.K. under the title
DESERT DOCTOR, SECRET SHEIKH.

Copyright © 2008 by Meredith Webber.

www.eHarlequin.com

Printed in U.S.A.

CLAIMED BY THE
DESERT PRINCE

CHAPTER ONE

JEN lifted the almost weightless child onto her hip and turned towards the car approaching them, hoping the driver would stop before he reached the tents so the cloud of gritty sand the vehicle was kicking up would settle outside rather than inside her makeshift hospital.

He did stop. The battered four-wheel-drive pulled up some twenty metres from where she stood, but a perverse drift of wind lifted the trailing red cloud and carried it in her direction, so she had to step backwards in order not to be engulfed in its dust. She put her hand over the little girl's nose and mouth, and scowled at the man stepping out from behind the wheel.

Unexpected visitors usually meant trouble. Most of the small states in this area had moved quickly into the twentieth century and then the twenty-first, with modern cities, wonderful facilities and the best of medical care, but in Zaheer, the ruling sheikh did not agree with modern ways and though he himself was rarely seen, his minions made the presence of even essential aid services uncomfortable.

The man who disembarked wore rather tattered jeans and a T-shirt, not the flowing robes of the usual official sent to ask what they were doing and to be shown around, suspicion of the organisation's aims bristling in the air.

This man was very different, though why Jen had that impression she couldn't say.

Was he a traveller lost in the desert, or something else?

Some instinct she'd never felt before warned her to be wary but she dismissed this vague unease with a sharp, unspoken *Nonsense!* Beneath the dust on the vehicle there appeared to be some kind of logo, so maybe he *was* an official, or an aid worker from another organisation.

She wanted to ignore him, to turn away, tired of the battles she fought with red tape, but with more refugees arriving at the camp every day she needed all the help she could get, and he might just be helpful to her.

She stood her ground.

But she didn't smile.

Which was probably just as well, she realised as the man stepped out of his dust cloud and she caught her first good look at the tall, well-built figure, the tanned skin, the dark, dark hair and—surely not green eyes?

She looked again as he came closer—they *were* green, pale, translucent almost, and so compelling she knew she was staring.

But all in all he was a man women would stare at automatically, and smile at as well—probably to cover the fluttering in the region of their hearts.

Not that she did heart flutters over men—not since David…

'Dr Stapleton?'

The visitor's voice was deep, but with a huskiness that suggested he might have a cold or sore throat, or that he might have cultivated it—a bedroom voice, practised for seduction…

Seduction? Where had that thought sprung from?

'Yes!' she managed, nodding to reinforce the spoken confirmation, knowing the fleeting thought of danger was nonsensical.

'I'm Kam Rahman,' the stranger said, stepping closer and offering his hand. 'Head office of Aid for All heard you were in trouble—trying to look after the medical needs of the people in the camp as well as run the TB programme—and sent me along to look into setting up a medical clinic here and to investigate the needs of the refugees.'

'You're a doctor?' Jen asked, taking in the threadbare jeans and the T-shirt that looked older than she was, once again trying not to be distracted by the blatant maleness of the body inside them.

'Trained in London,' he said, bowing deeply. 'But my father was an official of sorts in this country so I grew up here and speak the language, which is why Aid for All thought I'd be more useful here than in South America, where my language skills would be useless. Although, given the way the world works, it's a wonder I didn't end up there.'

He smiled, perhaps in the hope she'd enjoyed his little joke, but the smile made the sense of danger stronger and Jen found herself taking a backward step and shifting Rosana so the child was between her and the stranger.

Not that the man noticed her movement, or registered that she hadn't taken his proffered hand. He was too busy looking around, his keen eyes scanning the tent city that spread outward from the end of the road.

'You're more than welcome,' Jen told him, although inside she didn't feel at all welcoming. Inside she felt disturbed, which, she supposed, wasn't all that unbelievable because the man, with his erect carriage, his strong body, high cheekbones, the slightly hooded but miss-nothing green eyes, oozed sex appeal.

Startled by the directions of her thoughts, she realised it had been a long time since she'd noticed a man as a man, let alone considered whether he was sexy or not.

But there was something else about him that diverted her from personal reactions, something in his bearing…

Authority?

Now, why would she think that?

'So, are you going to show me around?'

The same authority in his voice, and it *was* authority—of that she had no doubt.

He'd thrust his hands into his jeans pockets, making the fabric tight around his butt as he turned, the better to see the extent of the camp, and Jen was distracted again.

Aware she should be thinking about the reason the man was here, not whether or not he had a good backside, Jen dragged her mind back into order.

'You're really an Aid for All worker—really a doctor?'

He turned back to her and smiled, which didn't help the disturbance in her body, then he crossed to the dirty vehicle and rubbed his hand across the passenger door to clear the dust from the logo.

'See, same as yours.' He nodded towards the equally dusty vehicle she and her team used. 'I don't have my framed medical graduation certificate with me—hard to hang things on the walls of tents—but I do have some ID.'

He plunged his hand into his pocket and pulled out a plastic-covered tag similar to the one Jen wore around her neck.

'There, we match,' he said, slipping the cord over his head.

Kam with a K, she noticed, but the ID looked genuine.

So why did she still feel wary about this man?

Because he was so handsome?

Well, if that was the case, she'd better get over it. The people in the camp needed all the help they could get.

'Come on, I'll show you around,' she said, as Rosana wriggled in her arms.

Jen looked down at the little mite, dark eyes huge in her thin face, stick legs bent with rickets, stomach distended from starvation. 'There isn't much to see, well, not in the medical tent. It's very basic. If you're setting up a general medicine clinic, maybe we can get another tent for it so we're not tripping over each other.'

She looked hopefully at the newcomer.

'I don't suppose you brought a tent?'

He was frowning at her—frowning angrily—as he shook his head, although she couldn't think why he should be angry.

Until he spoke.

'Weren't tents supplied by the government? Tents for the refugees as well as tents for the people helping them? Didn't I hear that somewhere?'

Jen shrugged.

'I don't know, although I have heard that the old sheikh has been ill for a very long time so maybe the country isn't running as well as it should be. And Aid for All certainly had a battle getting permission to test for and treat TB in the camp, so once we received the permission we weren't going to push our luck by asking for more. The tent we use was housing a family when we arrived, and they moved out so we could have it.'

Kamid Rahman al'Kawali, heir to the sheikhdom but travelling incognito through his country, shook his head as he looked around at the tent village. Things were far worse than he and his twin brother Arun had imagined. And they had to take at least part of the responsibility, for they'd pretended not to notice what was happening in Zaheer, throwing themselves into their hospital duties, telling themselves their medical work was more important than disputes between government officials, changing what they could change at the hospital where they worked, but slowly and cautiously. They'd been constantly frustrated in their endeavours because, even ill, their father had been strong enough to refuse to hand over any authority to his sons.

So they'd worked, and learnt, attending conferences and courses all over the world, finding good excuses to not visit their father until the last possible moment when they'd come out of duty to their mother, not out of concern for an irascible old man who had made their childhoods a misery, and who had refused to move with his country into the twenty-first century.

He had despised the city that had grown where the old capital had been, the new city built by foreign oil barons made richer by the oil they pumped from beneath the desert sands, and by foreign hotel chains who had built luxury housing for the oil barons.

He had objected to the idea of his country becoming a democracy, although when he realised it was inevitable he had made sure his brothers and their sons had stood as candidates and been elected to look after the interests of the family. Then he'd hidden himself away in the fastness of his winter palace, the hereditary, but not ruling, ruler, allowing those in the far-off city to do as they wished. That aim seemed to be to make the city more prosperous, not to mention glamorous enough to be attractive to foreigners, and to ignore the fate of the rest of the country.

Which was why a foreign aid organisation was now testing for TB in a tent in this refugee camp near the border of the neighbouring country, while in the city, in nearly new hospitals, first-class surgeons recruited from around the world were performing face lifts and tummy tucks not only on women but on men who had become soft and flabby from indulging in their wealth.

Foreign aid! How could this have happened when the whole basis for the tribal life of his people was looking after their own? And the people in this refugee camp, although they may have come in from over the border, were still their own, descendants of the same tribes that had roamed the desert for centuries.

Kam sighed and looked at the woman in front of him. The smooth skin of her face, framed by a dark scarf, was lightly tanned and sprinkled with freckles that had a look of casually scattered gold dust to them, while her eyes were a darker gold, brown, he supposed they'd be called, but so flecked with golden lights the brown was hardly noticeable. Pink, shapely but unpainted lips, slightly chapped—had no one told her the dry desert air could suck all moisture out of you in a few hours?—were pursed by worry or concern…

And why was he suddenly so observant?

With so much to learn and so much to do to right the wrongs of the past, this was no time to be noticing a pretty woman…

'I can get tents,' he said.

'Just like that? You can get tents?' Jen demanded. 'I've been sending messages to the city for months now, saying we need more help— Oh!'

She lifted her hand and held it to her mouth—to stop herself putting her foot further into it?

'You *are* more help,' she muttered, then smiled tentatively at him. 'I'm sorry I haven't been more welcoming. But tents?'

Kam returned the smile.

'Influence in the city—I grew up here, remember.'

He was fascinated by the freckles but knew he shouldn't stare, so he let his gaze rove casually over her, then smiled once more to cover the fact that his attention had been so easily diverted.

Again!

'Tents are easy.'

Jen didn't miss his casual scan of her body, but she refused to blush, although she was only too aware of what a sight she must present, her Western garb of jeans and a long-sleeved shirt covered by a long, all-enveloping grey tunic, red desert sand coating it and probably her face as well, and turning her blonde plait, beneath her headscarf, a dried-out, gingery colour.

But his inspection of her apparel—and his apparent dismissal of it, although she had attempted to adapt her clothing to meet the customs of the land—had annoyed her sufficiently to go on the attack

'Good, and if you've that much influence, I'll make a list of other things we need.'

He held up his hand.

'Best if I work it out for myself,' he said. 'After all, I know these people and can assess what will suit them, while you might be imposing Western needs on them.'

'I would think clean water and sanitation would be basic needs for anyone,' Jen muttered, but she suspected he was right as far as details were concerned.

'Of course, and these things, too, can be provided,' he assured her.

'And perhaps better housing before the worst of winter blows along the valley,' Jen suggested hopefully.

He looked around and Jenny tried to see the camp through his eyes—the motley collection of patched and tattered tents, the tethered goats, the children running down the alleys between the dwellings, a small flock of ragged-looking sheep grazing on the lower hillside, while two hobbled camels slept nearby.

He shook his head.

'Housing? I don't think so. These people are refugees from across the border, this isn't their country. If we build them houses, aren't we telling them that they will never return to their own lands? Wouldn't we be taking away their hope?'

He was extraordinarily good-looking and it was distracting her, and the distraction made her snippy. Although she could see where he was coming from, she wasn't ready to give in too easily.

'You don't want these people who have lost everything to have some comfort and a proper place where they can be treated while they are ill?' she demanded.

'I would love them to have comfortable homes and a hospital as well, but back where they belong—back where they grew up and where their families have roamed for generations. Back in the places of their hearts! Here, surely, if we build something resembling a permanent camp, they will feel even more lost, displaced and stateless. It's like saying to them, "Give up all hope because the war will never end in your country so you'll just have to sit here on the edge of ours and live on whatever charity can provide." I doubt there are people anywhere in the world who could accept that, let alone these fiercely proud desert inhabitants.'

'Well, you obviously know best,' Jen said, turning away

from him towards the big tent and adding under her breath, 'Or think you do!'

An anger she couldn't understand was simmering deep inside her, although she didn't know what had caused it—surely not this man pointing out something she should have known herself? And surely not the passion that had crept into his words as if he truly understood, and possibly felt, these people's yearnings for their home?

No, passion was to be admired, but there was something about the man himself that stirred her anger, an air of—could it possibly be arrogance?

Kam turned away to speak to a man walking past and Jen took the opportunity to check him out again.

A number of doctors, like a number of professionals in any field, were arrogant, but they usually weren't dressed in well-worn jeans and tattered T-shirts. They were more the three-piece-suit brigade.

She sighed. She hated generalising and here she was doing it about a stranger—and about other members of her profession.

And why was she thinking of him as a man—noting his looks and manner—when she hadn't thought that way about a man since the accident—hadn't ever expected to think about a man that way again?

She reached the opening at the front of the tent, and turned to wait for him to catch up, while once again a sense of danger assailed her.

'This is where we work and where I live. You can have a look in here then I'll find someone to show you around the camp so you can get your bearings.'

He looked as if he was about to argue, but in the end did no more than nod and follow her into the tent.

She led the way, still holding Rosana on her hip, trying to see the place that was clinic, hospital and home through his eyes. Various bits of it were partitioned off by bright woven rugs she'd bought from the traders who came regularly to the camp, determined to get whatever money they could from the desperate refugees.

In the clinic corner, the morning ritual of TB testing was going on, men, women and children all coughing obligingly into tiny plastic cups, while one of Jen's local helpers spread the sputum onto a slide and labelled it with the patient's name.

'As you probably know, the refugees are mostly mountain people,' she explained to her visitor, 'driven out by the warring tribes across the border, and by starvation because with the war going on they can't plant their crops or take their live-stock to good pastures.'

Her guest—or should she start thinking of him as her colleague?—nodded.

'I imagine in these overcrowded conditions diseases like TB can spread quickly, and with complications like AIDS in some cases, your first priority must be to complete this eradi-cation programme.'

Maybe she *could* think of him as a colleague.

It would certainly be easier than thinking of him as a man...

'Except that things happen, of course, to get us off track,' she explained. 'A child gets too close to a fire and is burned, a woman goes into labour—naturally we have to tend them. In these people's eyes—and in reality, I suppose—we're a medical team, so they come to us for help.'

And though still wary of him—of the person, not the doctor, she decided—she gave him the welcome she should have offered in the first place.

'For that reason it's great to have you on board. You can do the normal medical stuff and we'll get on with the TB programme.'

'TB treatment involves a period of nine months.' He interrupted her so firmly she took a step back. 'You intend being here that long?'

He spoke with a hint of sceptical suspicion that fired the simmering embers of the anger she didn't understand to glowing life.

'What do you think? That I'm playing at being a volunteer? That I came here for some kind of thrill, or maybe kudos—so people would see what a wonderful person I am?'

She scowled at him.

'Of course I'm here for the duration of the testing and treatment, although it might not be a full nine months, but then again, with more people coming into the camp all the time, it might be longer than that.'

He was obviously unaffected by scowls, or scorn, or anger. He waited until she'd finished speaking, then asked, 'Why not a full nine months?'

'Because we've cut treatment time to six months through a selection of different medication,' she told him, tilting her chin so she could look him in the eyes. 'Once someone is on the programme it's mainly a matter of supervision to make sure they take their medication. Isolation would be good, if there was somewhere we could send those with the disease, but then again, to take these people from the few family they have left would add to their problems. We treat the physical things as we can, but the mental burden they carry—the sadness—we can do nothing for that.'

The visitor stared at her as if she'd suddenly begun to speak in tongues.

'And you care?' he asked.

Jen stared at him in disbelief.

'Of course I care. Why wouldn't I care? I presume you're here because you care, too, or is this some ruse? Are you some kind of government spy sent here to see what's happening in the camp, or an Aid for All spy, checking I'm not selling the TB drugs on the side? Is that why you're here?'

'I've told you why I'm here,' he replied, all cool arrogance again. Maybe it was the voice—so very English.

Rich English.

Was his father a foreign oil baron that Kam had grown up here? Or, in spite of that English voice, did the blood of a long line of desert warriors run through his veins? She'd learnt enough of the local people to know they were a proud race.

Although the questions kept popping up in her head, or maybe because of them, Jen ignored him, setting Rosana down on a mat on the floor and nodding to one of the women helping with the TB testing to keep an eye on the child. She was about to show him the layout of the tent when she became aware of approaching excitement, the shrieks and wails and general hysteria coming closer and closer.

Stepping past her visitor, she was heading out of the tent when he pulled her back, pushing her behind him and telling her to stay there.

As if she would! She moved up to his shoulder so they exited the tent together, and saw the excited crowd, a body held between a number of men, women shrieking lament behind them.

'He was thrown over the fence. Men on horses threw him. It is Lia's husband. They have beaten him with whips.'

Mahmoud, one of many men in the camp who spoke a little

English, explained this as the group moved closer, and as Jen stepped to one side and waved to the men carrying the patient to bring him inside, she heard her visitor cursing quietly beside her.

But cursing didn't help. She led the men behind a partition in the tent and indicated they should put their burden down on a plastic-covered mattress on the floor. Then she knelt beside the man and saw the blood-soaked, tattered remnants of his gown, in places sticking to his skin, on others torn right off. They turned him on his side, as the wounds were on the front and the back of his chest and on his calves. Jen found a couple of cushions she could prop behind his knees to keep him in that position.

The man was moaning piteously, but when the stranger spoke to him in his own language he found the strength to answer.

Jen, meanwhile, was wondering where to begin.

'Pain relief before we start to examine him, I think.' Her colleague answered her unspoken question, kneeling on the other side of the man but looking across him at Jen. 'What do you have?'

Jen did a quick mental scan of her precious drugs.

'I've a small supply of pethidine but we should run it through fluid in an IV for it to work faster.'

Fluid—she had so little in the way of fluid replacement, a couple of bags of isotonic saline solution and a couple of bags of five percent dextrose in water, which was also isotonic. The man had bled a lot and both would help restore plasma levels and though she hated using up what few supplies she had, she knew she would.

Was she frowning that her colleague, who'd been taking stock of the patient's injuries, now turned his attention to her?

'You *do* have some fluid?' he asked, and she nodded and stood up, asking one her assistants, Aisha, to bring a basin of water and cloths to bathe the man, before heading for the little partitioned-off section of the tent that was her bedroom and digging into the sand in one corner where she'd buried this treasure.

'You bury it?'

She turned to see Kam standing near the rug she'd hung to provide a little privacy to this area, and now *he* was frowning, although she was the one disturbed to have him in her space.

'To keep it safe from thieves.'

He shook his head and walked away.

Tubing, cannulas and catheters were buried in another part of the area she looked on as her room, and she dug them up and dusted sand off the plastic bags in which she'd buried them.

'I don't have much IV fluid replacement,' she said, when she joined him by the patient. She was angry with herself for sounding apologetic, but he merely shook his head, though he frowned again as he saw the sand dropping from the bundle she was unwrapping.

If frowns were any indication, he was one angry man...

'And what you have you must hide? Isn't that overdoing things? Do you feel you can't trust these people? How can you help them if distrust is in the air all the time?'

Anger sharpened the demands.

'I don't hide things from the people in the camp,' Jen told him, defending the refugees, although she knew some of them might steal from need. 'But raiders come from time to time. Even if they don't need medicines themselves, they can sell them. It's one of the reasons drug-resistant TB has spread so widely. People steal the medicine, sell it to unsuspecting locals in the souk, and never tell the buyers they need to take far more than one box of tablets in order to be cured.'

She knelt beside the patient, opening the small trunk that held their most used medical needs, like antiseptic and swabs and small sutures. She found what she needed and first bathed the man's left hand then swabbed it, before bringing up a vein and inserting a cannula into it.

Marij, Jen's other assistant, had passed a blood-pressure cuff and small monitor to Kam, who was now checking the man's BP and pulse, while Marij and Aisha were cutting off the tattered remnants of the man's robe, leaving pieces that were stuck to open wounds, which would be removed later.

Jen set up a drip, pulling a wooden box that had once contained TB drugs close to the man so she could sit the bag of fluid on it, then she broke open the ampoule of pethidine, drew the contents into a syringe and injected it into the fluid, adjusting the flow so their patient would receive it slowly over a prolonged period of time.

But as more and more of the man's clothing was cut away and Jen saw the depth of some of the wounds, she began to wonder if they would be able to help him.

'How could anyone do this to someone else?' she whispered, awed by the ferocity of the attack.

'They must have taken him for a thief or, worse, a spy,' Kam said, his voice grim.

'But—'

Once glance at his stern, set face stopped further protest and she reminded herself she was there to help, not to judge. She concentrated on their patient.

'I suppose we can only do what we can,' she said, thinking how little that might be—what if there were internal wounds they wouldn't know about until too late? Although now she had someone with whom she could work, maybe they *could* save this patient.

The visitor nodded.

'I know you're a TB clinic but would you have surgical instruments? I think if we can debride some of the damaged skin, there'll be less likelihood of infection.'

Jen thought of the odds and ends of instruments she'd acquired over the last three years, now packed in among her underwear in the battered suitcase in her makeshift bedroom.

'I'll get what I have,' she said, but as she rose to her feet she wondered why Kam Rahman didn't have all this equipment himself. If he *was* from Aid for All and coming here to run a medical clinic in conjunction with the TB clinic, surely he'd have brought supplies and equipment with him.

She glanced his way but the badge he'd shown her was now tucked inside the T-shirt. Later she'd take a closer look at the logo on his vehicle—better by far than thinking about digging under the T-shirt for his ID…

CHAPTER TWO

WHY was she suspicious of him? Because he was far too good-looking to be an aid worker? Did she have preconceived ideas that they all had to be long-haired and wear sandals and not speak like an English prince? As she considered these questions, she stacked all the instruments, sterilised by boiling and now wrapped in paper, on a battered metal tray and carried it out to put it beside the stranger, then suggested Marij empty the bowls of water and bring fresh.

'That's some collection,' Kam said, as Jen unwrapped her treasured instruments and set them on the tray where they could both reach them.

'Three years of humble begging,' she joked, but from the way his lips tightened he didn't think it was at all funny.

Which it probably wasn't but, then, there wasn't much to laugh about here, so the man had better loosen up and get used to feeble humour or he'd frown his way into a deep depression.

'Sutures?' he asked.

They were in the chest with the dressings—and fortunately she had plenty of them, mainly because they were the first things people pressed on her back at home when she visited hospitals or surgeries, asking for donations.

'Now, how are we going to work this? Do you want to cut and swab and I'll stitch or would you prefer to stitch?'

Jen stared in horror at the damage that had been done, not only to the man's back but to his chest as well. In places the lash, or whatever had been used, had bitten so deeply into his flesh she could see the grey-white bone beneath it.

'I'll cut and clean,' she said, and heard something of the horror she was feeling in the tightly squeezed-out words.

'He'll be all right,' her colleague said, his voice gentle as if he knew she was upset. 'It looks far, far worse than it really is. And with me to stitch him up, there'll barely be a scar.'

'Surgeon, are you?' Jen teased, though it was unlikely a specialist would be deployed to somewhere like this camp.

'And why not?' he parried, leaving Jen to wonder…

He spoke again, but this time to the patient, the slightly guttural words of the local language rolling off his tongue. The man opened bleary eyes then closed them again, and Kam nodded as if satisfied the drug was working.

'Let's go,' he said, and Jen started at the neck and began to cut away the cloth that was embedded in the wounds, preserving what skin she could but needing to debride it where it was too torn to take a suture. Desert sand encrusted the wounds and the blood-hardened fabric, so the job was slow, but piece by piece she removed the foreign material, leaving a clean wound for Kam to stitch.

From there she moved to the wounds just above his buttocks, so she and Kam weren't jostling each other as they worked, and slowly, painstakingly, they cleansed and cut and stitched until the man's back resembled a piece of patchwork, sutures criss-crossing it in all directions.

Jen squatted back on her heels and Kam raised his head,

tilting it from side to side, shrugging impressively broad shoulders to relieve tension in his neck. For a minute the green eyes met hers but she couldn't read whatever message they might hold. Pity? Horror? Regret?

Emotion certainly, and she felt a little more kindly towards him. So many doctors, surgeons in particular—and she was pretty sure he must be one—could remain detached from the work they did, believing it was better for all concerned for them to be emotionally uninvolved.

'Do you want to swap jobs?' Jen suggested, as Kam roughly taped a huge dressing to the man's back then tilted him so he was lying on it. They both watched the patient to see if there was any reaction, but as he remained seemingly asleep, they assumed the pethidine was working and he couldn't feel the pain of the wounds on his back.

'You've been bent over there for over an hour. I can at least move around,' Jen added.

He glanced at her again.

'You like sewing?' he asked.

'Not really,' Jen said, wondering how he could make her feel so uncomfortable. He was, after all, just a colleague.

Problem was, of course, she'd never had a colleague who looked like this one…

Or felt any physical reaction to a man for a long time…

She hauled her attention back to the subject under discussion. 'But I've done most of my hospital work in A and E, so I've had plenty of practice.'

She was sounding snappish again and knew it was because it niggled her that this man could get so easily under her skin.

Because she was physically attracted to him?

Balderdash! Of course she wasn't.

'I'm sure you'd do as good a job as I, but now I've begun I'll finish it.'

And finish it he did, Jen cutting and cleaning, Kam sewing, until all the deepest wounds on the man's back, chest and legs were stitched, while the less deep ones were neatly dressed.

Jen, finishing first, checked their patient's blood pressure and pulse again, then studied the readout with trepidation.

'His blood pressure's dropping. I saw you examining him all over earlier—there were no deep wounds we've missed?'

Kam shook his head.

'But there's extensive bruising to his lower back and abdomen, which suggests he might have been kicked. There could be damage to his spleen or kidneys and internal bleeding, which we won't find without an X-ray or ultrasound.'

'Do you have a radio in your car? Do you know enough about the health services available locally to know if we could radio for a helicopter to take him out?'

Kam shook his head.

'I imagine you drove in, camping out in the desert for one night on the way. That's not because we—I mean the locals—want to put aid workers to as much hardship as they can, but because of the mountains around here. They have temperamental updraughts and downdraughts that can cause tremendous problems to the rotors on a helicopter, so they don't fly here. Fixed-wing aircraft are a different matter, they fly higher so aren't affected, but, of course, there's no handy airfield for even a light plane to use!'

He studied her as if to gauge her reaction to his explanation, but when he spoke again she realised he'd gone back further than the helicopters.

'You asked about a radio in my car—yes, I do have one,

but so should you. One in the car and one for your office or wherever you want to keep it—they're listed on the inventory you're given with your supplies.'

Jen smiled at him.

'The one in the car disappeared within two days of our arrival and the other one a couple of days after that. You can't dig a hole and bury radios. No matter how well you wrap them, you can't seal them completely and they tend to stop working when sand gets into their bits.'

She was smiling at him, but Kam couldn't return the smile, too angered by the artless conversation. He couldn't believe that things had got so bad people were stealing from an aid organisation, although he imagined these refugees had so little, he could hardly blame them for the thefts.

But how to fix this? How to redress the balance in his country? Could he and his twin achieve what needed to be done in a lifetime? Arun was working in the city, talking to the people there, seeking information about the government and whether, as their father's influence slipped, corruption had crept in.

Or had the people elected into positions of power only seen the city as their responsibility, ignoring what was happening in the country, ignorant of this camp on the border?

As he and Arun had been, he reminded himself with a feeling of deep shame. He couldn't speak for his twin, but nothing—neither work and study programmes, nor his father's orders to keep his nose out of the ruler's business—excused the way he, as heir, had allowed neglect to hurt his people. And nothing would stop his drive to fix this hurt.

Nothing!

Their patient groaned and Kam brought his mind sharply back to the job in hand.

'A drop in blood pressure certainly suggests he's bleeding somewhere. If you're short of fluid, we should consider whole blood.'

The woman he'd been surprised to find in this place nodded. He'd known she was here, of course, but he'd expected...

What?

Some dowdy female?

OK, not some dowdy female, but definitely not a beauty like this golden woman was. He checked the dusting of freckles again and even in the dimmer light of the tent saw the colour of them.

'Sorry?' Checking out her freckles, he'd seen her lips moving and realised she was talking to him.

'I was just offering to take some blood from him and test it, then maybe find some volunteers willing to be tested,' Jen suggested.

'His friends will surely volunteer. Take some blood. You can test it here? You have a kit?'

She nodded.

'Good,' Kam said, pleased his mind was back on the job, though the greater job still awaited him. 'We've got him this far, let's see if we can finish the job. Internal bleeding will sometimes stop, leaking vessels sealing themselves off, but if it doesn't, without an ultrasound I'd have to open him up and have a look. He's suffered so much already I wouldn't like to risk it until he's much stronger, so let's wait and see. We'll have to monitor him closely, of course.'

We'll have to monitor him? The words echoed in Jen's head.

The stranger intended staying?

Here?

In her tent?

Of course he intended staying—he was another aid worker, one who was sorely needed, and right now there wasn't another tent to house him or his clinic.

Unease fluttered like panicking moths in her stomach—or maybe that was hunger, it was well past lunchtime.

She turned her attention back to the job she was supposed to be doing—taking blood.

Marij had returned, having belatedly finished the morning's TB testing.

'Can I help?' she asked, in her soft, gentle voice.

'Would you type this blood for me?' Jen asked her, handing her the vial.

'Of course,' Marij replied, adding, 'And then you'll want volunteers—I will ask around and begin typing them as well.'

Jen turned her attention back to the patient.

'Shall we ease him back onto his side? And what about antibiotics? I have some but they're in tablet form. For a start at least, he should be getting them through his drip. And tetanus? Who knows if he's ever had a tetanus shot, but if it was a horse whip he was hit with, he'll need one.'

He helped her move the patient back onto his side, propping cushions gently against his injured back to keep him from rolling over.

'I've stuff like that in the car,' Kam said. 'Not much because this visit was more a recce to see what was needed, but I'll go and get what I have.'

Once again suspicion fluttered in Jen's chest. Would he really undertake a two-day drive just to see what was happening? And then drive back to the city to get what was needed and drive up here again? Six days going back and forth across desert roads that could swallow a car whole?

Or was the flutter discomfort at the thought of the man moving his things in here—moving in himself?

So close that if she woke in the night she might hear him shifting in his sleep, hear him breathing?

But where else could he stay? Until they had another tent, and she'd believe he could muster one when she saw it, he'd have to live and work here. If she put up another rug across the far corner…

She shook her head at her own folly. Whatever it was about this man that was affecting her, it wasn't going to be stopped by a brightly woven rug hung down between them. The way they blew when the tent sides were rolled up to allow cool air in, another rug would barely provide privacy.

She checked her patient, then looked up as a shadow fell across them. The cause of her concern was standing over them, a large cardboard box in his hands.

Was she staring that he offered a half smile?

The flutters she felt were definitely not suspicion, and all the more worrying because of that.

'I have some more pethidine,' he said, such an ordinary conversation, 'and antibiotics. The blood test?'

'Marij is checking now.'

Jen climbed carefully to her feet, but even with care she stumbled when she put her weight on a foot that had gone to sleep.

Kam's hand reached out to steady her, his grip surprisingly strong. She turned to thank him, but the words wouldn't come, held captive in her throat by something she couldn't explain.

She stamped her unresponsive foot, and caught his lips curving into a smile.

'That's not a sign of a tantrum,' she assured him, with a tentative smile of her own. 'The darned thing's gone to sleep. And so's my brain. I know you introduced yourself earlier, but did I? My name's Jenny.'

She held out her hand and watched him take it—saw the tanned skin of his fingers against her own pale flesh, felt warmth and something else—something she didn't want to put a name to.

'I knew the Jennifer part, but wondered if you shortened it.'

Jenny removed her hand from his, and tucked it in the pocket of her tunic, out of danger's way.

'Jen, Jenny, even, hey, you—I answer to them all,' she said, trying desperately to sound casual and light-hearted, although her arm where he had touched it, and the fingers he'd briefly held, burned as if they'd been branded.

The patient's name, they learned, was Akbar, and his blood group was B.

'Mine's B,' Jenny told Kam, who was sitting, cross-legged, by their patient, talking quietly to Lia, Akbar's wife. 'Let's do a cross-match and see if it's OK for him to have mine.'

Kam studied her for a moment, wondering about this woman he'd found on the border of his country. Wondering if she was the first fair-haired Westerner to ever tread these particular desert sands.

Wondering if he should take her blood...

Take *her*, as his ancestors might have...

The sudden heat in his body shocked him back to the matter in hand. Of all the times to be distracted by a woman...

'You need your strength for your job,' he objected.

It was a token protest and she took it that way.

'The loss of a couple of pints of blood won't hurt me,' she

insisted, handing him a syringe with a needle attached so he could draw blood from her forearm for cross-matching. She had pulled off her soiled tunic and now rolled up the sleeve of her shirt so he could access a vein, yet he felt strangely reluctant to move closer to her—to touch her.

He *had* to move closer—how else could he withdraw some blood?—and if their patient was bleeding internally, and his blood pressure drop suggested he was, he would need blood.

Kam crossed the distance between them in one long stride and took her arm, seeing as he did so pale scars like snail tracks, paler than the lightly tanned skin and puckered here and there.

Without regard to the intrusiveness of the gesture, he ran his forefinger lightly down the longest of them, then looked up into her eyes, knowing she'd read the question in his own.

Defiance was his answer, as clear as if it was written on a whiteboard. Ask me if you dare, she was saying, and though Kam knew he shouldn't, he couldn't help himself.

'Accident?'

She nodded briefly then swabbed the spot where a vein showed blue beneath the fine skin of her inner elbow.

Take the blood, she was saying with the gesture—take the blood and mind your own business. But Kam's mind was already racing off along a tangent—did the scars explain why such a beautiful woman, and she *was* beautiful in her golden, glowing way, would hide herself away in a refugee camp on the edge of a little-known country?

Was she hiding only these surface scars or were there deeper ones?

Had she lost someone she loved, leaving scars on her heart?

'Was it bad?'

She stared at him as if she didn't understand his question, but a shadow had crossed her face and he had his answer.

Very bad, that shadow told him, while the set of her lips again warned him off further questions.

But his sympathy for her made him gentle as he held her arm and eased the needle into the vein. He watched the vial fill with dark blood, trying to keep his mind on the job—on their patient and what might lie ahead for him, and for himself and Jenny as his doctors—not on snail-track-like scars on a woman's arm, or the dark shadow that had crossed her face.

Fortunately, the woman—Jenny—recovered her composure and her sensible conversation brought him back to the present.

'If it works in a cross-match, you can take it directly from me to him, although you'll have to keep an eye on him for any transfusion reaction because I'll be lying beside him.'

She smiled as if this were a little joke at her expense, but Kam couldn't return the smile, his thoughts veering back to the puzzle of why this woman was willing to do so much for people she didn't know, in an inhospitable place, and with no friends or family to support her.

Had she come to escape her memories?

Her pain?

'Well?' she prompted. 'Are you going to do a cross-match or should I?'

With his mind back on the job, Kam took another vial and drew a little blood from their patient, Jenny acting as nurse, tightening the tourniquet on the man's arm to bring up a vein then taping a dressing over the small wound. Kam mixed the contents of the two vials, watching anxiously for any sign of clotting, which would tell them the blood samples were not compatible. But the blood didn't clot and the intrepid woman who puzzled him now produced a cannula and loop of tubing.

'Let's go,' she said, sitting down beside Akbar while one of the nurses who worked with her explained to Akbar's wife what was happening.

Lia shifted to sit beside Jenny and hold her hand, babbling her thanks for the gift of blood—the gift of life.

'You need to be higher,' Kam told the unexpected donor. 'Are you all right to sit up if we stack pillows behind you?'

'I've two bedrolls behind the partition,' Jenny told him. 'I can sit with those behind me to prop me up and that way my arm is higher than Akbar's and it will feed down into him.'

She half smiled, while the nurse, Aisha, fetched the bedrolls.

'It will be up to you to check the blood's going the right way. I don't want to be taking more of it from the poor man.'

Not only was she here in this desperate situation but she was joking about it. Kam thought back to the women he had studied with, both women from his own land and Western women, but none of them had been anything like this particular female doctor. No fuss, no nonsense, just get on with the job.

Although there *was* one problem now he thought about it…

'I don't think we should run it direct into Akbar. We should measure the amount—both for your sake as a donor and his as the recipient,' he said, trying to be as efficient as she was at getting on with the job. 'Do you have a container?'

'The fluid bag is nearly empty. What if we run my blood into it, a pint at a time, then transfer it across to Akbar? We could fill something else, but at least we know the bag is sterile. And we can time it, so we know how long it takes to fill a bag then do away with that middle stage when he needs more.'

Kam realised he should have thought of these things. Had

he become too used to have everything he needed for his work right at his fingertips—too used to modern medical practices—to think laterally?

Setting the questions aside, he did as she'd advised, siting the cannula carefully into Jenny's arm, feeling the slight resistance as he pushed the needle through her skin then withdrew it carefully from the cannula, leaving the tube in place. He let this fill with blood before closing off the fluid running into Akbar and replacing that tube with the one through which Jenny's blood was running.

He switched the tubes again and began running the precious red liquid far more slowly into the patient. And he *did* watch for a reaction, feeling Akbar's skin, already hot with the beginnings of a fever, probably caused by infection, seeking other signs of transfusion reaction like violent shivering. But Akbar's body gave no indication that the stranger's blood was upsetting him. He lay still and barely conscious and hopefully would remain that way for some time, below the level of pain, while antibiotics and the body's natural defences began to heal his wounds.

'As if such wounds could ever heal!' Kam muttered to himself, but his second patient had heard him. 'To be beaten must be the height of humiliation,' he added, to explain his thoughts.

'We can only do so much,' Jen reminded him, as they sat and watched in case there was a delayed reaction. 'We can get him physically well, then hope that love and support and his own determination will get him the rest of the way.'

This was too much altogether for Kam—the woman was too good to be true. There had to be a catch, some reason she'd hidden herself out here, hiding her body under all-enveloping clothes and her golden hair under a scarf.

Surely this was taking escape too far!

'Why *are* you here?'

In this, his land, such a question was extremely rude, but Kam asked it anyway, wanting to know, although uncomfortable with his curiosity.

'To run a TB eradication programme,' she replied, a tiny smile flickering about her lips. 'We've covered that.'

'But why *here?* There must be people in your own land who need medical help. Your accent says you're Australian—isn't that right?'

She nodded, but her gold-brown eyes looked preoccupied, as if she'd never really thought about answers to his questions before that moment.

'I do work in the outback at home as well,' she finally told him. 'One placement at home, then one overseas.'

She paused, studying him for a moment as if deciding whether she'd elaborate on this answer or not.

What had she seen that she spoke again?

'I actually like the foreign placements better. At home, I feel a sense of helplessness that I will never be able to do enough, as if my efforts are nothing more than one grain of sand in a wide desert—scarcely seen or felt, and certainly of no significance. But here, and in other places I've been—in Africa, in Colombia—I feel whatever I do is helping, even if it's only in a very small way. And I do particular projects, like this TB programme, that have a beginning and an end.'

This time her smile was wider, and her eyes gleamed as if in offering him a confidence she was conferring a present on him.

'I look on these trips as my reward.'

Kam saw the smile but her eyes, not her lips, had caught,

and held, his attention. Hadn't someone once said that the eyes were the mirror of the soul? In this woman's eyes he'd seen compassion, and pain for their patient, and now a gleam that suggested a sense of humour.

Which she'd certainly need out here.

But still he was intrigued. 'So, working, moving on—that's what you like. Is it the freedom? The lack of ties to one particular place or person?'

She studied him for a moment, then she nodded.

'It's what I like,' she confirmed.

'You are a very strange woman.'

Her smile broadened.

'A very ordinary woman,' she corrected him. 'Some people see the things I do as noble or self-sacrificing but, in fact, it's totally selfish, because I love doing it—love the adventure of going somewhere different, the challenge of meeting goals under sometimes trying circumstances, the fun of learning about another culture, meeting people I would never have met if I'd stayed at home, tucked safely away in a GP practice, seeing people a hundred other doctors could see and listen to and treat.'

Kam was checking Akbar's pulse as Jenny explained this, but his disbelief registered in a quick shake of his head.

'And is there no one left behind you who is harmed by your adventures? No one left to worry?'

He turned to look at her, certain she would tell the truth but wanting to watch her face where, he was sure, he'd read hesitation if she chose to avoid his question.

'My parents are both GPs, in a safe practice, one I might one day join, but although they wouldn't choose to do what I have done, they live vicariously through my travels. They support me and scrounge equipment and drugs for me, and take in strangers I send to them, people from distant lands who need more medical attention than I can provide. They had a Guatemalan family live with them for six months while local reconstructive surgeons fixed their daughter's face. She'd been born with a double hare lip and cleft palate.'

Kam shook his head again, unable to find the words to express his surprise, although his own people would take in those in trouble just as easily. But he'd always considered that the way of the desert, born out of need when the support of others might make a difference between life and death.

'Let's see if the blood is doing any good. I'll check his blood pressure.'

The woman's practical suggestion jolted him as his mind had wandered far from his patient.

'I keep forgetting we don't have monitors doing these things for us all the time,' he admitted

Jenny smiled and shook her head.

'No such luck. But before they had all these fancy things, doctors managed and so will we.'

Kam returned her smile.

'Of course we will.'

He watched as she inflated the blood-pressure cuff and they both watched the readout on the small screen of the machine. Akbar's blood pressure hadn't dropped any further, but neither had it risen.

'Let's give it an hour,' Kam suggested. 'Are you feeling all right? Would you like a break from this tent before you give the second pint? A walk or, better still, a cup of tea? What eating arrangements do you have? It seems a long time since I had breakfast at my campsite.'

'A cup of tea and something to eat is easily fixed,' Jen said as he put out a hand to help her to her feet.

She took the offered hand reluctantly, no doubt because of the uneasiness and flutters, but she was grateful for it as he steadied her.

'This way.'

Telling Aisha where she'd be, she led Kam towards the food tent, squaring her shoulders and walking straighter as she recalled his upright posture and the slightly arrogant tilt of his head, wondering again about the blood of desert warriors...

The food tent was set up by a different volunteer aid organisation and stocked with tinned and dried foodstuffs. Most of the refugees collected food from the canteen but cooked and ate within their family groups, but those who had no families now ran the tent as a kind of cafeteria, providing hot water for tea and coffee and meals three times a day.

'Smells good,' Kam said as he entered.

'Stew,' Jenny explained. 'Not made with goat but with canned corned beef and dried vegetables. It tastes much better than it sounds.'

'Or you get very hungry out here in the desert and would eat anything,' her companion said, and Jen suspected he was teasing her. But would he tease, this stranger with the profile that could have been used as a model for an artist to etch an emperor's face on an ancient coin?

She had no idea and was slightly concerned that she'd even considered it because teasing, even gentle teasing, felt like personal attention...

The women tending the big kettles and stew pots handed them small glasses of tea and indicated they should sit while the bowls were filled with food.

Jenny lowered herself easily, used by now to this custom of sitting on one leg while the other was propped in front of her to use as an arm rest as she ate.

'You adapt quickly to local customs?' Kam said, half-teasing again as he nodded at the position she'd taken up.

'These people have had thousands of years to work out the best way to sit while eating—why would I want to do otherwise?'

She sipped her strong, sweet tea—the sugar was added as the water boiled—and watched the shadow of a smile pass across his face, then he too sipped at the steaming liquid, raising his head to speak in another tongue to the woman who was putting food in front of him. Jenny knew they were words of thanks and praise because, rather than the guttural sounds of everyday talk, they had the soft, musical notes that, to Jen, always sounded more like spoken poetry than day-to-day language.

'I may be able to sit properly,' Jen told him, 'but no matter how hard I try, I can't get my "Thank you" to sound like you make it sound. I think it would take a lifetime to learn the Arabic language.'

'And another lifetime, or two or three, to learn different tribal variations of it,' Kam told her. 'I can probably make myself understood to the people of the camp, but every tribe has words that are common only to it. Do you know that in Arabic there are eight hundred words for sword, three hundred for camel and two hundred for snake?'

'Putting the sword—an instrument of death—at the top of the most useful word list?'

He studied her for a moment then smiled a real smile, one that lit up his rather stern face and revealed strong, even white teeth.

'Definitely not. They have even more words for love.'

The huskiness was back in his voice, and Jen shivered as a strange sensation feathered down her spine.

She glanced at her companion, hoping her reaction hadn't been obvious to him, and was pleased to see he'd turned his attention to the woman serving their meals, speaking again, perhaps telling her how good the food smelt.

Another of the women set a bowl of food in front of Jenny and handed her a thin round of bread.

'Eat,' she said, then smiled shyly, as if embarrassed by showing off the English word.

Jen returned the compliment by thanking her in Arabic, although she knew her pronunciation was hopeless—especially after hearing Kam's fluid, rhythmic use of the same words.

They ate, Jen now adept at scooping up the food with her bread, holding it always in her right hand and using pieces of it as easily as she'd use cutlery at home. But as she ate uneasiness crept in, born of not knowing what to make of the stranger who already seemed so at home in the camp.

'We shall check on our patient then sit outside for a while,' he decreed, as if picking up on vibes she hadn't realised she was giving out. 'Today's experience has probably made you think of other things that a proper medical clinic will need.'

'I refuse to think about work while I'm eating,' Jenny said, wiping the bread around her bowl to soak up the last bits of gravy. 'Especially as we haven't had dessert yet.'

As she spoke one of the women approached, a big metal dish of sheep's milk yoghurt in her arms. She scooped some into Jenny's bowl, handed her a spoon, then passed her a tin of golden syrup, a carton of which had somehow found its way into the camp's supplies.

'Best dessert in the world,' Jen told Kam, scooping golden

syrup onto her yoghurt. 'Sweet and sour and very yummy. The women here think I'm mad!'

He watched her eat, shaking his head when the woman offered him yoghurt and Jenny urged the golden syrup on him, but she'd only taken a couple of mouthfuls when Rosana appeared, crawling across the floor of the tent and settling herself into Jenny's lap. Now Jenny shared, spooning most of the treat into Rosana's mouth, cuddling the little girl and talking to her all the time, although she knew Rosana didn't understand a word she said.

'She has no family?' Kam asked as they left the tent, Rosana once again perched on Jenny's hip.

'Not that we can find. In fact, I think she might belong to one of the warring tribes or clans across the border.'

She paused, stopping beneath a spindly juniper tree, knowing questions could be considered rude but intrigued enough to ask anyway.

'Having lived here, grown up here, do you know enough about these countries to understand the war that is going on over there?'

CHAPTER THREE

'SUCH a simple question,' Kam replied, 'but it's like asking me to tell you the history of the Bedouin in a couple of sentences. You know they are the nomadic tribes that roamed the deserts of the Arabian peninsula and north Africa, although in Africa there were Tuareg as well.'

His listener nodded, but it was the intensity in her eyes—her genuine interest and what seemed like a need to know—that spurred him on.

'Originally people think there were three main tribes, but over the years these divided into many clans. Clans and tribes were headed by sheikhs, who were appointed by the elders of the tribe, although members of the one family were usually the ones chosen so in a way leadership was hereditary.'

'And have they always fought or is it only recently that wars like the one over the border have been going on?'

Kam smiled at the ingenuousness of the question.

'They've always fought,' he admitted. 'Often against invaders, especially infidels, but also against each other, one tribe sending hundreds of men on camels and on foot to raid another tribe's camels. But the fighting had strict rules. You never attacked at night because Bedouin believe a man's soul leaves his body at night and to attack then would be to attack a dead man. So they would attack early in the morning, which gave the men who'd lost the camels all day to give chase and maybe recapture their own stock.'

'Giving them a sporting chance? It sounds more like a game than serious warfare,' Jenny said, smiling at him.

To encourage him to keep talking?

Or because she was relaxed and happy in his company?

He gave a long inward sigh that he should even think such a thing. The problem was, he'd been too long without a woman, not wanting, since he'd returned to practice in Zaheer, to have the complications of a love affair while establishing himself at the hospital. Then there'd been his father's illness and the suspicion that all was not well throughout the land, although until their father's death, he and Arun had been unable to do anything about it.

Now they could, but first they had to know what needed to be done, hence his decision to visit the more remote areas. Once they had a clear picture of what was happening, they could plan for the future, and do what they could to right past wrongs and bring better conditions to the whole country, not just the city.

Another smothered sigh, because thinking of Arun had reminded Kam that between them they had to work out the succession. It would probably have to be him, he knew this in his heart. As well as being the elder, he doubted Arun would ever marry again, and children were important to their people and to the succession.

Very important!

Arun's first wife, the gentle and beautiful Hussa, had died from complications of a burst appendix. Arun had been in the city, and his bride had been too shy and ill at ease in her new home in the family compound in the country to mention to anyone that she felt ill.

Arun had been devastated, but once over the loss had become a playboy, courting and escorting beautiful women of every nationality, determined to enjoy life his way but equally determined to remain unmarried, no matter how the women he bedded used their wiles.

But he, Kam, was talking warfare, not women, although thinking of Arun and Hussa and the succession had reminded him of another matter he had to sort out—that of finding a wife. As Zaheer's ruler it was his duty to marry, and though he'd once dreamed of marrying for love, love had never found him, so now his mother was actively pursuing a wife search on his behalf...

Definitely better to think of history and camels and raiding parties than wives and marriage—besides which, Jenny was looking at him as if puzzled by the lengthy pause in his explanation.

What had he been saying?

Battles...

Camels...

'It *was* serious, because camels were a tribe's wealth, but it became more serious when the tribes began to give up their nomadic lifestyle and settle in one place. In the past, tribes usually had a set pattern in their wanderings, spending summer months in one place and winter months in another, roaming from area to area, but within certain boundaries, to find grazing for their camels.'

'And sheep and goats?'

'Sheep and goats? My dear woman, the true Bedouin acknowledged only camels and horses. He might buy a goat from a village where goats were raised, and cook it up for a special feast—the birth of a son, for instance—but camels were their stock, providing all they needed—meat and milk, hair for making clothes and tents. You have seen women spinning camel hair?'

The woman shook her head and the moonlight caught the paleness of her plait as it shifted with the movement, catching his eye as well, making him wonder what the hair looked like unbound...

Was it because right now he should be sitting with his mother, discussing his requirements for a wife and checking the list of candidates, that he was distracted by the sight of pale hair?

'Where was I?' he asked, and even to his own ears it sounded like a demand, but Jenny stood her ground.

'The nomadic tribes settling in one place.'

Her face displayed her interest—a strong, intelligent face—but he wasn't going to be distracted again.

'Of course,' he continued smoothly. 'Across the border here you have two clans, both of the same tribe, both claiming to own the land where they want to settle. It is an impossibility to grant rights to one or the other because ownership of land has never been part of Bedouin history. The people here in the camp are from a different tribe, and the only thing the clans across the border agree on is that this particular tribe shouldn't be there, although, in fact, they have had their camps in the area for many hundreds of years and recently many of them have settled in the area, breeding sheep and goats.'

'So how will it be resolved?'

'Men from other clans within that tribe are already talking to the leaders. They need to settle the dispute soon because like all wars it means no one's planting crops or keeping herds and soon there'll be an even worse famine in the area. I understand people have already tried to mediate, but at the moment no one is listening.'

He paused, looking at the little girl who was perched on Jenny's hip, her head resting trustingly on the woman's shoulder, her eyes closed in sleep.

'As you said, she probably belongs to one of the clans across the border. The family would have known she was sick and that she would be better cared for here.'

Jenny brushed her fingers across the soft dark hair.

'Poor wee mite! But she's a favourite with everyone so she's never short of people to take care of her. She probably eats better than anyone else in the camp, although as you can see that hasn't always been the case.'

'Yet she comes to you at night? Is it wise that she should become dependent on you? Learn to love you? And you, if you love her, then leave…'

Jen stopped and breathed deeply, relishing the feel of the cool night air entering her lungs, enjoying the smell of the desert—of sand, and dust, and flowers she couldn't name, and goat and camel and juniper trees.

But tonight there was another dimension to the magic, and try as she may to deny it, it was to do with a man in jeans and ancient T-shirt…

A man who spoke of love…

'Is it ever wise to love? Yet we all do it,' Jen replied, dropping a kiss on the child's dark hair. 'Opening ourselves up to the vulnerability it brings with it, and to the hurt and anguish when it ends. You must know that, for when you spoke of the history of the Bedouins and the tribes just now, you spoke with passion. Growing up here, learning the history, it's obvious you grew to love this place.'

He was walking again, and she followed, realising he was heading towards a flat rock ledge where she often sat herself at night, looking out at the desert, purple in the darkness, the waves of the dunes reaching all the way to the horizon like the ocean on a windless day. Here she enjoyed the wide, star-bright sky and the wash of the cooling night wind over her skin. Here she felt, if not happiness then at least something that was very close to it.

He turned as he reached it.

'So you are an expert on love in all its manifestations?'

The question was so unexpected Jenny waited until she'd sat down to consider it.

Not that it took much consideration.

'Definitely not,' she said. 'I doubt anyone is. Although if you've experienced romantic love, then you might think you know about it. As for the other kind, love for each other, that's easier, although there are always people you come in contact with whom you can't love, even though some are people that your friends and family might find extremely lovable. But an expert, no way! What triggers love within us is a mystery to me.'

Was she really sitting here, looking out over the vast sandy desert, talking about love with a stranger?

'With romance, it's physical attraction, surely,' her companion said, not looking at her as he spoke so she had a moonlit view of his profile.

'Maybe that's what brings people together to start off with, but it doesn't always turn to love,' Jen argued. 'Look at all the marriages that break up, the affairs that end. Maybe love should come before the physical attraction—start with common interests and friendship and let love grow from that, not from over-heated hormones or a rush of testosterone to the brain.'

She saw him smile but he didn't answer for a moment, and when he turned towards her the smile was gone.

'So maybe the ways of the people here are wise, in that a bride is chosen based on suitability, not attraction. In olden times a bridegroom rarely met his bride before the wedding day—or days as it used to be—although he may have known her as a child, because marriages were made within the tribes and clans so she could have been a cousin he'd played with when he was young.'

Jen knew he was explaining more of the local customs and history for her benefit, yet she heard a note of…sadness, or perhaps inevitability in his voice.

'You speak as if you're not sure if you approve or disap-prove of that particular custom,' she said, hoping for another smile, but all she got in answer was a shrug of broad shoul-ders before he turned back towards the desert stretched out in front of them.

Discomfited by the silence, Jen turned the conversation back to their patient.

'Getting right off love for the moment, if Akbar has internal bleeding, what's it most likely to be? Spleen?'

Kam looked at her and nodded as if agreeing with the change of conversation, or at least accepting it.

'I would think that's the most likely. It's easily damaged and will bleed a lot but on the good side it will often cure itself or, worst case scenario, he can live without it.'

Jen couldn't hold back her gasp of horror.

'You'd operate on him here? Remove his spleen? Under these conditions?'

Once again she had his attention and once again he was smiling.

'Wasn't it you who pointed out that doctors in days that are not so distant managed all these things without all the modern equipment we have on hand today.'

'They patched people up and hoped they'd live,' Jen protested.

'Which is what we'll do if we have to,' Kam said, his voice brooking no argument. 'What do you know about him?' he added, just in case she intended disobeying the warning in his voice. '*Did* he go to commit robbery that he was so severely beaten?'

'I'm guessing he went to find his son, although he may not have told his captors that, fearing for the safety of the child,' Jen explained. 'I know Lia has been distraught about the loss of their little boy. Apparently he was playing at a friend's house when they fled and they thought their friends would also flee and bring young Hamid, but when they arrived neither the boy nor their neighbours appeared.'

'They could all have been killed in the first raid,' Kam murmured.

Jen shook her head.

'Apparently not. The neighbour's wife was from a different tribe—from the tribe that is now in control of that area—so custom suggests she'd be spared and no doubt the boy is still with her.'

'Women and children have always been spared,' Kam told her.

'Or so men say,' Jen reminded him. 'But are they spared, left at home while their husbands and sons go out to fight? What are they spared? Physical injury, which is all very well, but line that up against mental anguish. I don't think they're spared much.'

Kam Rahman turned towards her, something like a scowl marring the stern symmetry of his features.

'You are the most argumentative woman I have ever met,' he said, and she had to laugh.

'That's not arguing,' Jen protested. 'That's nothing more than not agreeing with you! Have you reached such lofty heights in your career that lesser minions in the hospital bow and scrape to you? People often do to surgeons.'

But if he *was* a top surgeon, or even a middle-ranking one, what was he doing here?

Suspicion once again seeped beneath Jen's skin and she studied the man who sat looking out at the desert.

'You're right,' he said, surprising her by agreeing. 'The women do suffer. I wonder if that's why they are more superstitious than men, believing in amulets and written words that can ward off the evil eye.'

'Ah!' Jen said. 'I've wondered about that. Some of the women ask Marij or Aisha to write a word or words on a piece of paper and it is then tucked into a leather bag they wear around their necks. I thought they must be prayers.'

'They are,' Kam said, 'because who better to protect them than their God, whatever name he uses?'

But he wasn't thinking about amulets or prayers but that the women in the camp could not write. For whatever reason they were here, on the edge of his country, they should be being helped, and taught, a school set up for the children and perhaps informal lessons for the women.

Could he achieve all that was needed? How much could one man—two if he counted Arun—do to right perhaps not wrongs but certainly neglect? And how quickly could he set things up? The urgency of the situation struck him and with it came the knowledge that he couldn't afford to be distracted by his attraction to this chance-met stranger.

'I can understand their prayers, when they have so little,' Jenny said, breaking into his thoughts of what might lie ahead. 'Yet they do seem to have hope. I can't explain it in words but it seems to me that all these people hold hope in their hearts. Hope that soon they can return to the lands they know—to their summer camp in the wadi where the dates grow, or their winter camp where the cliffs are honeycombed with caves carved out by their ancestors over centuries. Those with English talk about it all the time and you don't have to be here long before you begin to feel this longing, or hunger, or need, all around you.'

But Kam already understood. Deep in his own Bedouin blood were the urges of migration, the need to feel the desert sands beneath his feet and to roam the lands his ancestors had called their own.

He frowned at his companion. His family had been settled for many generations now, and in spite of his father's intransigence about moving into the modern world, all his children and his brothers' children had been sent overseas to study, to become modern men and women.

Look at him—a doctor, a specialist surgeon!

So how could this woman stir a longing for the desert in his blood? How could she make him wonder if he needed an amulet or a word written on paper in a bag around his neck to protect him from her wiles?

Yet they weren't feminine wiles she practised...

Or were they?

He studied her, sitting so still on the rock, the child cradled in her arms. Just so had men and women sat all through the ages, he imagined, in this place—on this rock—but they would be a family, man, woman, child, so this was nothing but an illusion.

Yet it was an illusion he found unsettling…

As he found the woman unsettling.

He thought back to the list he'd given his mother—a list of the attributes she would look for in his wife—quiet, gentle, amiable, supportive, home-loving, a good housekeeper, equable and attractive had headed the list, and although he'd added intelligent and educated, both he and his mother had wondered if such additions were necessary. This woman would qualify for the last two, and was more than attractive, even when coated in desert dust, but as for the rest…

He shook his head in answer to his own question. This was a woman with wanderlust in her blood and a longing to keep moving on.

The silence didn't bother Jen for she loved looking out over the desert sands, but the peace she usually found at these times eluded her. Tonight the cool air brought tension with it, brushing new sensations against her skin and making her feel edgy, twitchy, uptight…

She tried to analyse these feelings, hoping that naming them might make them go away. But dissatisfaction was the closest she could come and she knew that must be wrong. She was in a magical place, doing a job she loved, so where would dissatisfaction come in?

Rosana grew heavy in her arms, and Jen shifted.

'I must take her in and put her to bed, then check our patient,' she said, and was surprised when Kam rose first, stepping towards her and lifting the sleeping child out of her arms.

'Sit there a while. It will do you good. I'll give the child to Marij or Aisha to put to bed and check our patient for you.'

Jen stared at him, trying to read whatever thoughts his face might reveal in the clear light of the moon. But as she hadn't been able to read it by daylight, trying now was futile, though as he bent to lift Rosana from her arms he was close enough for her to see the strong bones in his cheeks and the high dome of his forehead—the dark eyebrows above the unexpected eyes, and the smooth, tanned skin that was wrinkled at the corners of his eyes. From smiles and laughter, or from growing up in the strong sunlight of this country, squinting in the desert sun?

He took the child and Jenny watched him walk away. She'd seen little evidence of smiles and not heard laughter from him, so maybe they *were* sun-squints!

She propped her back against a rock and looked out at the rolling dunes, trying to think of things she needed for the camp that this man might provide, but his image kept rising up in her mind and she couldn't push it far enough to one side for her brain to work on practical problems.

Although she *had* written a wish list not long after she'd arrived. She'd concentrate on that—picture the words on paper. A well—that was the first item on her list. She knew from her reading that many wells had been drilled in the desert—water wells to provide a permanent water supply for the Bedouin who still roamed the land.

But would an Aid for All worker know influential enough people to have a well drilled at the camp?

He was walking back towards her, so now would be a good time to find out. Better to talk about wells and a new clinic than to sit in silence, surrounded by the magic of the desert, and allow this man's presence to move towards her on the breeze and stroke her skin and send shivers down her spine.

'Do you think it would be possible to get someone, the government maybe, to drill a well to provide a permanent supply of water for the camp? At present we get big bladders of water trucked in and we ration it, but we're not always sure where it comes from and some bladders seem to be less clean than others. Everyone knows they should boil it before using it, but whether they do…'

He frowned down at her, then sank down in one easy motion to sit, cross-legged, on the rock.

The silence chafed Jenny's nerves, forcing her into more conversation.

'Of course, there mightn't be underground water so drilling a well could be useless.'

A deeper frown, clearly visible in the moonlight.

'There should be water,' he finally replied. 'Underground rivers run from the mountains—the wadis where the dates grow are fed by them. In the wadis the water is closer to the surface and easier to get to.'

There ended the conversation, no agreement or otherwise to asking someone to drill for a well. In fact, it seemed to Jenny that he'd moved far away from the fairly trivial conversation and was now lost in contemplation of things she couldn't guess at.

She studied his face as he looked out over the desert. She read sadness in it, but resolve as well, then she shook her head. Who did she think she was, judging a man's feelings from his facial expression—especially a man she didn't know and whose expression was verging on impassive?

But her thoughts had broken the magic of the evening so she broke the silence, pushing him on the subject they'd been discussing.

'Well?' she prompted, then had to smile that she'd used the

word in another sense, but if he saw anything amusing in it
he certainly wasn't showing it, still frowning at her.

'You are sitting here with so much beauty all around you
and thinking of wells?'

'We were talking earlier of what was needed in the camp,'
she reminded him, although she couldn't remember if they
had been talking about it or if she'd introduced the topic to
distract herself from personal thoughts and feelings.

He waved a hand in her direction.

'The well is negligible—it will be done.'

He shrugged as if he could have a team of well-drillers here
by morning, so insignificant he considered it, but it made
Jenny even more suspicious of him. There was something
going on here that she didn't like, but she couldn't work out
what was bothering her.

Apart, of course, from the attraction she was feeling for this
man—attraction she'd thought she'd never feel again.

'And if you wish to spoil the beauty of the evening with
practicalities, I have been thinking we could ask for a couple
of portable buildings—the ones that look like shipping containers. The oil companies use them for the workers living on
site when new oil wells are being drilled. The buildings are
shifted on trucks. We could ask one of the companies to give
us one to use as a clinic-hospital.'

'Just like that?' she said, stunned by the size of the project
he was suggesting. 'Aid for All practically had to beg to be
allowed in to the country to do the TB programme with the
refugees, and now you're confident enough of local support
to produce a mobile clinic?'

She stared at him, again trying to read what he was thinking
in his face, although she knew she was only guessing.

But he did look sad—it had to be sadness, making the corners of his well-shaped mouth droop slightly at the corners and the skin between his eyebrows deepen into a black frown.

'The old ruler has died,' he said. 'Things are changing.'

'Well. I'm glad to hear that, but will they change fast enough for us to get a well and the clinic?'

'They will change,' he repeated, and it seemed to Jenny that the words were a vow of some kind.

But, then again, it could be the magic of the moonlight on the desert creating fancies in her head, or the spell of the man to whom she felt attraction, weaving words about her, snaring her, though unaware of the disruption his arrival had caused in her usually placid life.

She had to get away—from him and the beauty and the moonlight—had to collect herself and her thoughts and get back to being sensible, practical Jenny Stapleton, doctor and aid worker...

'I'll check on Akbar,' she said, standing up and walking away before Kam could argue. She ducked into the tent, which seemed very dim after the moonlight, although it was lit by a couple of bright gas lanterns. Kneeling beside the patient, Jen nodded to Lia who sat so patiently by his side, wiping his brow and face with a damp cloth and whispering little prayers or words of love.

And as she examined him, Jen told Lia what she was doing, although she knew the other woman would understand very few of the words. But how else to communicate? She usually managed through hand signs and smiles, often leading to laughter, but with Akbar so badly injured only the most reassuring of smiles had any place in the strange conversation.

He seemed feverish, and tossed uneasily in his sleep, but

with pain relief and antibiotics flowing into him, there was nothing more they could do. Except refill his bag of blood, which was nearly empty.

She took his blood pressure and found it had dropped further. There *had* to be internal bleeding, although his pulse was good. Low blood pressure from internal bleeding was usually accompanied by tachycardia, a rapid pulse, which made the two signs she was reading contradictory.

Would they have to have a look?

Jen shuddered as she imagined even attempting to operate under these conditions. And if they had to, would it be better to do it now, before he lost more blood?

A sound behind her made her turn to see Kam had followed her in. Jenny stood up and spoke her thoughts out loud, glad she had someone with whom to share her worries.

But Kam was having none of it, turning it back on her.

'If I wasn't here, what would you do?' he asked, and she tried to think, although thinking was hard when he was so distractingly close.

'I doubt I'd operate, not right now, and that's not entirely because I'm not proficient at surgery or that it seems ridiculous to even attempt it in these circumstances, but because sometimes waiting and watching is better than rushing in. Maybe whatever it is will fix itself. There's no distension of his abdomen, although I know he'd have to lose a lot of blood for that to happen, but there seems to be little tenderness either. I pressed my hands against each quadrant and though he murmured when I touched where deep wounds were, he didn't flinch away at any stage.'

Kam nodded his agreement. He'd like to examine the man himself but if he did it would look as if he didn't trust Jenny's judgement and he didn't want to hurt her feelings.

'I'd like to give him more blood, though,' she said, 'and see if that helps his BP.'

She paused, then smiled at him.

'And your fingers are itching to examine him, aren't they?' Her smile broadened, making Kam think of things far removed from medicine. 'Go right ahead, I've always believed in getting second opinions. Also, you can examine bits of him I wouldn't like to, not out of any prudishness but for fear of upsetting Lia, and Akbar himself if he became aware of it.'

He took her at her word and repeated the examination he was sure she'd done quite competently, in the end agreeing with her decision to do nothing yet. If Akbar's condition deteriorated further during the night, then they could and would operate, but the old medical adage of 'First do no harm' kept ringing in his head.

Was she pleased he agreed with her? He couldn't tell, maybe because she was fussing with the bedrolls and organising herself to give more blood.

So practical for such a beautiful woman, or was that a sexist thought?

But as Kam bent over her to uncap the cannula he'd inserted earlier and fit a tube to it, he couldn't help but wonder again what had brought her here.

Wonder also if she felt any of the attraction he could feel simmering in the air between them, or if it was all one-way— she attracting him.

If she knew that, or felt anything, then she was hiding it well, treating him with polite consideration, tinged with just a hint of suspicion, as if his explanation for his sudden arrival at the refugee camp didn't sit well with her.

CHAPTER FOUR

JEN settled back against the bedrolls, once again wishing Aisha or Marij had been here to take the blood, but Aisha had gone to her own quarters earlier, and when Jen had returned to the tent, she'd sent Marij off to bed, telling the nurse she would watch Akbar overnight.

So she had Kam, kneeling so close to her she could feel the heat of his body, and a tiny flare of inner heat she didn't want to think about…

'It is best it goes more slowly into him than it comes out of you,' he said. 'So we will fill the bag again, then you, too, will go to bed. He will be my patient for the night.'

'I can watch him for a couple of hours,' Jen replied. 'I have to check the TB samples and also put out the medications for tomorrow.'

'Now?' Kam asked, surprised by the woman's complacency when faced with another few hours' work after she'd given a second pint of blood.

He started the blood feeding into the empty bag, resting it on a mat on the floor so the flow wasn't compromised.

'Of course now,' she said. 'Well, as soon as this is finished. It's why we're here. For testing we take samples on three consecutive mornings then, if they're found to be positive, we start the patients on the drug regime. Because we can only test about thirty people a day, the camp is divided into sections. In Section One, all those with active TB have been on medication for a couple of months, while we're still testing people in Section Seven, which is where new refugees come in.'

Kam considered the logistics of this. The camp, from what he'd learned, had close to a thousand people in it.

'How many are you treating? How prevalent is it?'

'About two hundred and eighty at the moment. Some are at the beginning of their treatment, when we give them streptomycin for two months as well as the three drugs usually used for treatment, while others are four months in and only have another two months to go.'

'You use isoniazid, rifampicin and pyrazinamide?'

Jen nodded.

'We give them the lot daily for two months then cut back to twice-weekly doses of isoniazid and rifampicin for another four months. It's more expensive than just giving the isoniazid and rifampicin for nine months, but it cuts the time of the treatment to six months and it's easier to monitor the drugs over six months.'

'Because you have fewer people dropping out of the treatment over the shorter period of time?'

'That's the theory, but we still get dropouts.'

Was he really interested or just making conversation?

And why did it matter?

Jen couldn't answer that one but she knew it did matter.

Was it because of that tiny niggle of suspicion she felt towards him, or because she was attracted to him?

She didn't think she'd like the answer to either question.

'Dropouts?' the attractive but suspicious man prompted.

'I'm sorry, I was thinking of something else. What did you ask?'

'I wondered if the dropouts remained in the camp or if you have people going back across the border.'

'I think some go back, although maybe what's happened to Akbar today will put a stop to that for a while. But some join up with the traders and go down to the city on this side of the border.' She hesitated then added, 'Oh, dear, I suppose that makes them illegal immigrants. I shouldn't have betrayed them like that.'

Kam smiled at her.

'In these parts, the lines that make this our country and the other side someone else's were drawn on maps made of paper, but it's far harder to draw a line in sand. I would think the locals recognise boundaries for business purposes, but people are people and should be able to travel freely wherever they wish, especially the real nomads of the desert.'

'I couldn't agree more,' Jen said, liking him again, seeing his deep and genuine regard for the desert people and his common-sense approach to boundaries. 'And now the bag's full, isn't it? I'd better get to work.'

He detached the tubing and reattached the drip to Akbar while Jenny stretched and climbed back to her feet.

She walked across to the far side of the tent where another small gas light was shining on the wide bench where she'd examine that morning's slides, then make patient notes and write out the drug list for the following day. Marij and Aisha distributed the drugs, using a group of young boys to run around the camp to find anyone who failed to come in.

'What about contagion?'

She turned to see Kam had followed her.

'In crowded situations like this, is it not spreading faster than you can cure it?'

'I don't have any scientific proof, but it doesn't seem to spread once treatment's under way. We are inoculating people we know for certain don't have it as we go, so eventually it should be wiped out, in this community at least.'

'Eventually? Will you stay that long? Will you see this happen?'

Jen shook her head.

'I'll stay through all the testing and initiation of treatment, checking for adverse drug reactions in people starting treatment and finding other drugs for them if it proves necessary, but once everyone's been tested and checked, probably in another month, I'll leave Aisha and Marij to oversee the distribution of the drugs and move on to something else—somewhere else.'

'Always moving? You are running from something perhaps? A broken heart? A failed marriage?'

Jen turned to face him, angry that he should accuse her of such things.

Even if they might, in part, be true…

Surely not, not after all this time. It had been five years since the accident, five years since she'd lost David and their unborn child and she'd thought her world had ended…

'No. I'm running towards something,' she said firmly. 'This is work I love, work I do well, and while I can I will continue to do it. It gives me all I need, with adventure, challenge and fun, not to mention satisfaction. Later, as I grow older, I might become less effective and that will be the time to reconsider this lifestyle.'

She tilted her chin in case he hadn't heard the defiance in her voice. He was shaking his head, as if he didn't believe her, but which bit didn't he believe—that she loved the work, the challenge, the adventure, or that she would continue to do it?

Deciding she'd never know, and it was best to ignore him anyway, she worked her way through the slides and set out lists of drugs to be dispensed the following morning. Because the drug regimen changed after two months and also because the patients were at different levels of treatment, the lists were important.

She felt, rather than saw, Kam move closer, leaning over her shoulder as she checked and rechecked the lists.

'You number the patients?'

Was he criticising this method? She swung around to look at him.

'Aisha and Marij give out the medication, and they use the person's name, but it is too easy for someone like me, who doesn't understand the subtleties of the language to make a mistake, calling a man Mahmoud when his name is Mahood, or something else that to me seems similar. It could lead to disaster. We have another list of names and numbers for the nurses, but after a few weeks they know all the names.'

Jenny considered this a rational explanation, so why didn't the man move away? Surely he couldn't be fascinated by sputum slides?

But whatever was keeping him so close didn't matter— what mattered was how his presence was making her feel. Out on the ledge above the desert, she'd blamed the air—the cooling breeze—for the discomfort she had felt in his presence, but here, in the tent, there was no breeze.

'You do this every night? Write down the medication lists?'

'Of course. I'm responsible so it's right I should do it. The numbers make it easy for me as well, because we started with one so the patients who have early numbers are well into their treatment. By the time I leave, these early numbered patients will be finished, and that in itself is a reward.'

Now surely he would move away.

He did, but not very far, pulling a stool over to the desk and settling next to her.

'I'll do the slides,' he said. 'I'm looking for acid-fast bacilli, am I?'

Jen turned towards him.

'You don't have to do this,' she said. 'It doesn't take me long.'

'And you don't trust me enough that you won't check them after me? Isn't that what you're saying?'

He was sitting so close she could see the shadow of his beard beneath his skin, so close she could smell the desert and the wind on his clothes.

'I will check them again,' she said, 'not because I don't trust you, but because it's the way I work. We take three specimens because one doesn't always show bacilli, and I compare all three. If there are three clear slides we cross that person off, inoculate them against TB and that's the last we see of them. When we find infection the person gets a number and the drug regimen begins. So tonight I have to take these slides and compare them against the ones from previous specimens and although this table might not look as if it's organised, it is.'

She reached over in front of him and lifted a slide that had a dab of yellow paint on one corner.

'Yellow is the third day, so I find this patient's first and second day slides—red and blue—and put them all together.

Once all three have been checked they get tossed into a drum of antiseptic and later will be boiled up to be reused.'

She was talking too much, explaining things that didn't need explaining and really were nothing to do with him, but the uneasiness she'd felt since the man had first appeared was growing and her body was turning wayward on her yet again, responding to something he was giving out—unconsciously, Jen was sure.

She kept explaining.

Kam listened to her talk, not because the testing and treatment of TB patients held an irresistible attraction for him but because he found he enjoyed listening to her voice.

Was he, as his American friends would say, losing the plot here?

He'd come to check out what was happening on the far edge of his country and to see what could be done to help.

He'd also come because he had been inexplicably angry and not a little ashamed to find out a foreign aid organisation was at work out here, when surely his people should be looking after the refugees in the way desert tribes had cared for each other right down through the centuries.

Now, when there was so much to be done—and not only here—he was distracted...

By a woman...

He shifted back a little so as not to be so close—not to feel her warmth and smell the woman smell of her.

Which gave her room to move!

'Well, that's done. I'm off to bed.'

She stood up and turned towards him.

'Are you sure you want to watch our patient overnight? I can share the duty—with two of us, we won't have to do long shifts.'

'No, I will watch him,' Kam assured her. 'I sleep lightly so I can doze beside him. I think his wife, too, will wish to be close. Between us we will ensure he continues to be stable. But before that, can I do anything for you? The camp is quiet so I assume all your helpers have retired to their beds. Do you need water for washing? Can I fetch it for you?'

She turned towards him, a frown pleating her forehead.

'You don't have to do that, neither do my helpers. I know my skin's a different colour to that of the people I treat, but I do try to respect their customs of dress and behaviour so that they don't think of me as too different or outlandish. Women here are the water-carriers. I'm a woman and I fetch my own water.'

She paused then smiled.

'Although now and then a small boy will do it for me—or maybe not for me but for the lollies I give him as a reward.'

Kam didn't like the smile. Not the smile as such, for it was a very charming smile. What he didn't like was the effect it had on him. It made him feel warm, and stirred more longing in his blood, only this longing was not for the desert sands…

He should walk away—swiftly—but instead found himself speaking once again.

'Just this once, can you not think of me as a small boy? I won't even ask for lollies. You have a bucket or a drum? And the water…'

She smiled again, her lips twisting upward in a teasing kind of delight.

'I doubt even the most vivid of imaginations could put you into the small-boy category. We'll go together,' she suggested. 'Maybe that way my reputation as a woman won't be totally destroyed by having a man fetch my water.'

She slipped away, returning with a plastic container so big he wondered how she—or small boys—ever carried it.

He took it from her, his fingers brushing hers, and knew this was probably the most stupid thing he had ever done in his entire life. This woman, foreign, argumentative and stubborn as she was, had already cast some kind of spell over him but as yet it wasn't strong enough to hold him captive. Now every instinct told him that to walk out of the tent with her, to stand in the moonlight once again, would tighten the invisible bounds, perhaps inescapably.

Something had happened back there in the tent. Jenny wasn't sure what it was, but she could feel it in every cell in her body. It was as if their conversation about TB and drug regimens had only floated on the surface of their minds while beneath it some unspoken dialogue had been going on.

But what?

She didn't have a clue.

She suspected that it had to do with the flutters she didn't want to admit to, and the butterflies in her stomach, and the shivery sensation that kept running up and down her spine, although it was far too scary to admit that, even to herself.

But as they ducked out the entrance to the tent and stood again in the moonlight, she could feel—what? Magic? Hardly, but something indefinable in the air, as if this man's presence in the camp—and right now by her side—was changing the very essence of her life.

'How ridiculous!'

'Ridiculous?' he echoed, and she realised, to her embarrassment, that the words had burst from her uncensored.

'Well, not ridiculous.' She struggled to cover up. 'More unimaginable. Here I am on the edge of a desert country, surrounded by Bedouin tents, and goats and sheep, walking to fetch water with a stranger by my side. It's like all the fairy-tales I read as a child rolled into one. Weird!'

'Until we reach the waterhole and instead of it being a lovely oasis in which you can see your fair reflection, or a well from which pure spring water gushes, it's a black balloon that's dusty and leaking and probably full of bacteria. The well will come before long. I promise you.'

He sounded angry and she wondered if she'd upset him with her silly talk of fairy-tales, but as he filled the drum with water she sensed his anger was dissipating and as they walked back to the big tent he pointed out the constellations, naming the groups of stars that were foreign to her, here in the northern skies.

Kam carried the water back to the tent, following her behind the hanging rug into the area where she apparently lived. He was appalled by the poverty of it—not poverty in a monetary sense but the lack of facilities for a woman such as she.

'You don't have a bed, a table, or a chair?'

The words burst from his lips and, as she lit a small lamp and hung it on a long metal hook that dangled from the centre of the space, she smiled at him.

'Neither do the refugees in their tents,' she reminded him. 'But I have my bedroll...' she waved her hand towards the larger of the bedrolls which she'd used as pillows earlier '...my suitcase full of clothes, a box of books, a basin to wash in and my drums for water. What else would I need?'

Kam thought of his brother's women, and some women he himself had enjoyed in the past—considered their sumptuous, scented bedrooms and racks of clothes and shelves of beauty products. Even his mother, who was old-fashioned in many ways, had an ensuite bathroom off her room and a fantastic array of perfume bottles ranged along its shelves.

'You can live so simply?'

His voice betrayed his thoughts and the woman smiled.

'I've learned to,' she said. 'And learned to appreciate the simplicity of a life with few encumbrances, although,' she added, and he heard a trace of wistfulness in her voice, 'I sometimes hanker for a real bath—to lie back in the hot water, preferably with lots of bubbles breaking against my skin. In fact, it's the first thing I do when I get back to civilisation—I insist my hotel bathroom has a proper bath, not just a shower, and I indulge myself.'

To Kam's dismay an image of this woman in a bath popped up in his head and although he'd never seen her naked, he could picture her quite clearly, tall, lithe and lean, the bubbles she spoke of rising from the water, adding luminescence to her pale skin...

'Thanks!' she said, and he stared at her, sure she couldn't be thanking him for thinking of her naked. 'For the water,' she said patiently, reaching out to take the drum from his hand.

He dropped it to the ground, unwilling to let her fingers brush against his yet again, and left the room, if it could be called a room. But he couldn't escape the tent altogether for Lia was sleeping by her husband's side, and he, Kam, had promised to keep watch over the patient. So he settled himself on the mat beside the injured man and tried not to listen to the sounds of water being poured into the basin, or the soft, sloughing noises that suggested clothes being removed.

A scent, so subtle he didn't at first register it as something different, mixed with the smell of antiseptic. Did she have enough vanity to bring perfume with her after all? he wondered.

He glanced towards the hanging rug and saw her silhouette, as tall, slim and lithe as he'd expected, then shame crashed down on him and he turned away, unable to believe he'd betrayed her trust in such a way, but at the same time wondering how to suggest she change the place she hung the lamp. She might have other men in the hospital some time…

Jen pulled on the long, silky, dark blue, all-enveloping shift she wore to bed and unrolled her bedroll, then she sat on the mat beside it and unplaited her hair. She covered it with a scarf by day partly out of deference to the custom of the land but also because it was so difficult to wash it, out here in the desert, with the limited water supply. So, to keep some of the dust out and also to hide it when it badly needed washing, she was happy to cover it. But every night she brushed it, dragging out the tangles, getting rid of a lot of the sand it had collected during the day.

If she had one jot of sense she'd keep it short, but although she was willing to go anywhere Aid for All might send her, she couldn't bring herself to cut her hair.

Pride and vanity, she knew that's all she kept it for, but wasn't a woman entitled to a few of these vices? Like the rose-scented soap she carried with her to foreign lands. She might be bathing in dirty water, but the soap kept her feeling feminine.

Like her hair…

She brushed and brushed, not counting strokes but enjoying the relaxation the rhythmic motions provided.

Movements beyond the hanging rug reminded her she had company in the tent. A patient, his wife and a man she didn't want to think about, a man who, all too easily, had reminded her she was a woman.

Not that he had flirted with her in any way, but being near

him, talking with him, feeling the maleness of him brush across her skin, had stirred up sensations she'd thought she'd never feel again.

And brushing her hair was making things worse—it was such a feminine thing to do—

The cry was one of anguish and she forgot about hair and femininity and feelings she didn't want to acknowledge, reacting automatically, rising to her feet and hurrying into the front part of the tent, her hands twisting her hair into a coil and tucking it into a knot at the back of her head.

Akbar was tossing and turning, crying out words Jenny didn't understand. Kam knelt over him, holding him down, talking to him in a soothing voice that seemed to be doing little to lessen the patient's distress.'

'I have some pethidine in that box I brought in. Can you find another ampoule of it for me?' Kam asked Jenny as she dropped to her knees beside him. 'There are some there, they should be near the top. And draw it up to give him subcutaneously, which will work faster than an intramuscular injection. Once we have him back on fluid I can put the next dose, should he need it, in that.'

Jenny found the drug and thanked heaven Kam had appeared when he had, because without this narcotic analgesic to dull the pain and send Akbar back to sleep the man would be in agony.

She slid the injection into his arm, while Lia, who'd been woken up by her husband's cries, helped Kam restrain the angry, injured man.

Angry?

Was he remembering the beating? Jen wondered, squatting back on her heels as she waited for the drug to take effect.

Remembering the shame of it? Or was it just the pain that was upsetting him so much?

She glanced at Kam, wanting to ask him but knowing she couldn't—not right now.

But among the man's ravings she heard one word, repeated again and again—the man was crying not from pain but for his son.

A giant hand reached in and squeezed Jenny's heart, pain of loss remembered, pain she knew no narcotic, but only time, would heal…

Lia held her husband, tears streaming down her face, but she chattered on to him in a sing-song voice, trying desperately to calm the man she loved.

'Was it just pain upsetting him or is it the loss of his son? I heard him call the boy's name,' Jenny said to Kam, when Akbar had settled back into a drug-induced slumber and Lia once again lay quietly but vigilantly beside him. Kam had walked to the entrance of the tent and Jenny had followed him, needing to talk about the man's obvious distress.

Hoping it was pain, not loss!

Kam shook his head.

'It is being alive that's upset him,' he said quietly. 'He sees himself as a failure because he didn't find his son. He should have died, he was shouting, we should have let him die. He has no son, what is a man to do?'

'Are sons so very important?' Jen asked.

Kam looked surprised by the question.

'Of course. Every family needs a son to take care of the women should the father die. These days that might seem wrong, but the desire to sire a son is bred deep in the hearts and bones and blood of desert people.'

He paused and his face darkened.

'But in truth I believe Akbar feels a deep love for his son. Not all fathers are like that. For some the fact of siring a son or sons is enough.'

Was it thought of his own father that caused the flash of pain in his eyes? She found herself wanting to reach out and touch him, to comfort him, but right now the issue was Akbar, not of Kam's mysterious past.

'But if Akbar's feeling like that—as if he doesn't want to live—will we be able to save him? We need him fighting with us, not against us. Without his help, it will be harder to pull him through.' Now she was feeling Akbar's despair and knew Kam would hear it in her voice, but she couldn't hide it away behind empty platitudes or assurances.

'We have to get the boy,' she said. 'We haven't got Akbar this far to lose him because of despair.'

Kam turned towards the woman who'd spoken with so much determination. She was wearing a long, all-concealing gown yet he could imagine the shape of her body beneath it, while her hair, still golden in the moonlight, was sliding out of its knot and hanging in tendrils around her face.

Was she aware of her beauty? She must be. Surely no woman could be so devoid of vanity she'd not see how lovely she was.

'Negotiate some way. Do you know if they might need anything—the warring tribes? Food or water, maybe medicines? I wouldn't give them guns, but surely there's something we could offer for the boy.'

'I'm sorry, I was distracted.' Putting it mildly! 'You're not suggesting we meet with these people? The same people who have just beaten that man to within an inch of his life?'

'I'm not saying *we* as in you and I should, but you said

some tribal leaders were already talking to them in an attempt to stop the fighting, so maybe we could contact those people. Or I could go as a representative of—'

'Forget it!' Kam told her, sounding admirably calm considering how angry that final, ridiculous suggestion had made him feel. 'There is no way you are setting one toe across that border. I'm not saying those men are savages, but they consider themselves at war, and war doesn't permit a lot of niceties, neither does it have moral boundaries.'

He put his hands on her shoulders and turned her so she was facing him—so he could look down into her face and watch it and her eyes as he spoke.

'You will not go,' he said. 'Understand me?'

The cheeky grin that greeted this order raised his anger another notch.

'Understood, sir!' she said, and snapped a salute in his direction.

He was a man of the desert—he understood about straws and camels' backs—and that cocky gesture was one straw too many.

'You'd call me sir, would you?' he said softly, his body swaying closer to hers, into her space so she'd have to back away if she felt the threat implicit in his movement. 'And give me cheek, yet go on planning and plotting to get that boy back.'

He reached out and touched her cheek.

'You're thinking even now—will this work, will that?'

His fingers slid into the knot of hair and the whole arrangement came loose, sending the golden, silken threads cascading down her back.

'Will you use your beauty to beguile me? To include me in your plan? Is that the way you work, Dr Stapleton?'

He was close enough to see the golden flecks in her brown

eyes, and to see the rise and fall of her chest beneath her gown as she breathed in and out, in and out, perhaps a little fast.

'Will you offer me a kiss as payment?' Kam continued, sliding his hands beneath the heavy fall of her hair and lifting it to spread it around her shoulders. 'Will that work, do you think?'

Was she bewitched, Jen wondered, that she was held captive by his voice? Although witches did bewitching, not moonlight and strangers. In the desert there were peris, fairy-like creatures she suspected worked their magic by the light of the moon. Maybe they did spells…

'Shall we try?'

Some part of her head knew this was when she should break away—if not from the spell, at least out of reach of his hands and lips—definitely out of reach of those lips which were strong and firm yet so beautifully moulded she'd been sneaking looks at them on and off all day.

But her feet remained rooted in the cooling sand, and the man's face came closer, blocking out the moon, and finally his lips touched hers, brushing across them as softly as a night breeze before resting more positively, snaring hers and holding them captive as his voice had held her captive earlier.

There *had* to be a peri working magic somewhere here, because as kisses went it *was* magic. Not too demanding, nor too harsh, just a gentle but very thorough exploration of her lips and then her mouth while all the time his hand rested lightly on her back, beneath her hair, so at any time she could have stepped away.

But she may as well try to pull iron filings from a magnet. She couldn't move, content to have him explore, content to do a little exploration of her own, while her body went through the entire maelstrom of feelings she'd thought she'd never feel again—the tingling awareness, the fluttery beat of her heart, the slight queasiness in her stomach as if love was something for which there should be an antidote.

Although this was kissing, not love, and, if you considered that only their lips were touching—apart from the light hand on her back—it was very modest kissing at that. But Kam's lips…those lips had kissed before and were very, very good at it, which really should have been enough to make her step away but, alas, his expertise was also the reason why she couldn't.

'Do I sense you're not quite with me in this kiss?' he murmured, pulling far enough away for her to see his face. 'Please, tell me you're at least thinking about it and not about some mad scheme to get over the border and rescue the boy.'

She couldn't lie, so smiled instead.

'No, I was thinking about kisses,' she admitted, and saw the quick frown gather between his brows.

'Whose kisses in particular?' he asked, so huskily demanding she felt a sense of power, although she knew this man who barely knew her couldn't possibly be jealous.

'Oh, no one's in particular,' she said blithely, as if she'd sampled dozens and dozens of men's kisses rather than just David's. 'Just kisses in general.'

Kam growled then kissed her again, but this time the exploration stopped and the plunder began. This time he took and gave such heat and fire she thought her feet would surely leave scorch marks in the sand, and when he moved away she had to reach out for his arm to steady herself while her knees got organised enough to hold her up.

'We'd better say goodnight,' he said, his voice rasping against her lips as he kissed her one last time.

'We had,' she agreed, and, stronger now, drew away.

Tomorrow she'd ask Marij or Aisha about the peris and their deeds, or maybe this desert had its own spirits. Didn't djinns hail from these parts? Djinns, she knew, caused mischief, and could take on human or animal form. Was Kam a djinn in disguise, causing mischief in her life…?

CHAPTER FIVE

SHE woke up to noises in the tent, not cries and yells again but voices, speaking quietly, hushed in fact, as if the people out there didn't want to disturb her.

Slipping out of bed, she washed and dressed, glad she had a clean tunic to put on over her jeans, as she'd left the soiled one soaking overnight. Then, hair braided and scarf in place, she ventured forth to find Akbar still looking feverish and very pale, staring blindly at the roof of the tent while his wife and Kam spoke quietly beside him.

Jenny nodded to them but kept walking. Akbar wasn't one of her TB patients so she didn't know him well, and he might be a man who didn't want a woman, apart from his wife, to see him in this weakened state.

It was also better, she decided, to not be too close to Kam until she'd sorted out in her head exactly what had happened last night.

Well, she knew what had happened—she'd replayed it in every waking moment in the night. She'd allowed a virtual stranger to kiss her—worse, she'd kissed him back.

Eventually…

Embarrassment quivered in her toes and the distance

from her corner to the outer doorway of the tent seemed a million miles.

Kam, however, foiled her attempt at escape, calling her to the man's bedside and motioning for her to kneel down.

'Let me introduce you to Dr Stapleton,' Kam said to Akbar, who nodded regally towards Jenny as she knelt beside the mattress on the ground, then turned his head away. 'She, too, will be looking after you.'

Kam spoke in English first, for her sake, Jenny assumed, then repeated his words in dialect.

Akbar didn't respond, but Jenny sensed he hated the idea of being dependent on a woman and wondered if she could persuade Mahmoud or one of her other male volunteer helpers to act as his nurse. She'd talk to Kam about it—

'Come,' he said, as if she'd already mentioned needing to discuss something. 'We'll go to breakfast.'

He stood first, reaching down and taking her elbow to help her to her feet, and all the physical reactions she'd promised herself she wouldn't feel by daylight sparked through her body.

He *had* to be a djinn in human form!

Perhaps that would explain why he wasn't feeling any of the embarrassment she was feeling about the kiss.

Perhaps he'd already forgotten the kiss or, man-like, had put it out of his mind. Jen knew she wasn't a once-kissed-never-forgotten kind of girl but she felt slightly peeved to think he might have forgotten.

Duh!

She should be slapping her hand across her head to get her mind back on track, but as that might look a trifle weird, she made do with work-related conversation. After all, if Kam didn't remember the kiss there was no way in this wide world she'd let him know she did!

'Will Akbar find it hard to have women caring for him?' she asked as she walked beside, but an almost safe distance apart from, Kam towards the food tent. 'Should I get some of the men to take turns in sitting with him?'

'His friends will want to care for him, and most of them will take notice of what we tell them needs to be done, but we still have to watch for signs of infection and internal bleeding. I can do that. You're right, he'd prefer men around him.'

Kam sounded distracted and was frowning slightly, and she wondered if there was something he hadn't told her.

Or if, perhaps, he *did* remember the kiss…

But the conversation was medical, the subject Akbar, so she held up her end of it.

'I guessed as much. Well, as long as there aren't twenty of them clogging up the space and they don't bring their water pipes and smoke in there, I suppose I can put up with it.'

They'd reached the food tent where the women were already rolling up the sides so whatever breeze there was would flow through, but Kam had stopped and was staring at Jen as if he couldn't understand her words.

'You are one strange woman,' he said, and stood back for her to enter the tent.

Oh, yes? Had that judgement been made because she'd kept her distance—hadn't mentioned the kiss, and flung herself on top of him for another—or because she didn't want bubbling water pipes in her clinic tent?

She turned her head so she was looking back over her shoulder at him.

'Is that better or worse than argumentative?'

Kam heard the question, but didn't answer, mesmerised by something in the tilt of her head which had brought back memories of the previous evening. Instead of the woman in a dull grey tunic in front of him, he saw the woman in dark blue silk, her hair a second silken garment, a cloak around her shoulders.

'Argumentative, strange and stubborn,' he said, mainly to remind himself of the attributes that weren't on his list of what he wanted in a wife, although why he should be thinking of his potential wife in this woman's presence, he didn't know.

And how he'd gone so far as to kiss her, he had no idea. It wouldn't happen again, that was certain, for all she'd tasted like roses and honey...

The very last thing he needed right now was the distraction of a woman...

The woman in question was now speaking to the women in the tent, accepting a glass of tea then moving to where, to Kam's amazement, an array of breakfast cereal packets were lined up on a table.

'All this?' he said, waving his hand towards the choices.

'A breakfast cereal company is one of our largest contributors,' Jenny explained with a smile. 'I do keep telling their high-and-mighties that the basic ingredients—wheat and oats and corn—would be more acceptable and useful donations and far cheaper for them than giving us manufactured products, but I suppose grains don't have the brand name and trade mark stamped on them, so they lose out in advertising.'

'Advertising? They'd want to advertise their products way out here where no one has money to buy them, even if there were a shop from which they could?'

'Come and see,' Jenny said, laughing at him now, but she

took his hand and led him out of the tent and up onto a little ridge behind the camp. 'Look down,' she said, and the first thing he noticed was a cardboard patch on one of the tents, with the brand name of the cereal company written in huge letters across it. He looked around and here and there throughout the camp were similar patches.

'News planes fly over and take photos and what does everyone in the Western world see on the front page as they eat their cereal? Who knows, the letters are big enough they can probably see it from outer space. Martians might eventually come and visit earth for breakfast cereal.'

Kam smiled at her glib remark but inside he wasn't smiling. This was his country, albeit a very distant part of it, yet he was learning more about it from this foreigner than he could have believed possible.

And none of it was reassuring. Especially as the touch of her hand as she'd led him up the hill had distracted him again and he felt torn between his duty and this sudden and inexplicable attraction…

They returned to the food tent where he took a glass of tea, and ate cereal and yoghurt for his breakfast, pleased the organisation had scrounged spoons from somewhere so he didn't have to eat it with his fingers. They were sitting near the edge of the tent to get the breeze and his companion ate in silence for a while, then looked up at him.

'About Akbar, I didn't ask, was his blood pressure better this morning?'

'Much better, so if there was internal bleeding it seems to have stopped.' Kam thought this good news but his companion was frowning.

'But should we still take him down to the city for an ultrasound? You said you're here to look around and see what's needed—would you take him when you leave?'

'Let's wait and see,' Kam suggested. 'I don't need to return immediately, and if we keep an eye on him...'

Kam knew it was his own voice he was hearing, but what was he saying?

That he could stay in the camp indefinitely?

Of course he couldn't—there was far too much to see and do.

And why would he be thinking it?

He was looking at one possible answer, who was looking back at him with a puzzled expression on her face.

'But the well? The clinic?'

Kam waved his hand to dismiss her worries—and his own reservations.

'I can radio someone about them. I have a brother in the city—he'll find the right people to talk to about these things.'

Jenny grinned at him.

'If you still have a radio,' she teased, and Kam realised that although he'd been out to the car to get some gear, he hadn't thought to check.

'It had better be there,' he muttered, while his companion continued to smile, which infuriated him.

'And you should have one, too,' he growled. 'It's stupid to just accept that they are stolen and do nothing about it. What if something happened and you needed a radio in an emergency?'

'I think if it was life and death, a radio might magically reappear. There is no way on earth I'd show a lack of trust in any of these people by asking if they know where the radios have gone, but I wouldn't be surprised if at least one of them is in the camp.'

'And you just accept that? Accept the people you are helping would steal from you?'

Her smiled widened, lighting up her eyes, though there was sadness in it as well as she explained, 'They have so little, Kam, and have lost so much. If having a radio hidden in the corner of their tent makes up for even a millionth of the unhappiness they've suffered, I'm pleased for it to be there.'

He shook his head—he seemed to be doing it all the time, but every new thing he learned about this woman generated disbelief, while every new thing he learned about his country added to his sense of shame and frustration.

Of course he couldn't stay here for long, there were other outposts he needed to visit, camps along the northern wadi, small villages and towns. He had to learn about *all* the problems of his country, not just this corner of it.

But his body was remembering the kiss, weakening his resolve, although he knew full well it couldn't happen again. The very last thing he needed right now was a distraction and this woman, he suspected, could prove to be the distraction to end all distractions.

'I'll go and check I've still got a radio then have a look around the camp,' he said, as the little girl, Rosana, crawled into the tent.

But although Jenny picked her up and gave her a kiss and a cuddle, she then handed her over to one of the women who ran the food tent.

'I'll come with you as far as the car. We might meet a couple of my little boys on the way, boys you could trust to keep an eye on the car for you. If you explained to them you need the radio to let the people in the city know what is needed in the camp, I'm sure word would get around not to steal it.'

They left the tent together, but once outside Jenny paused,

as she always did, looking towards the mountains that rose up behind the camp, rough red and gold and ochre rock contrasting so magically with the vivid blue of the sky. She had come to love this particular view, and to feel connected to the mountains, so these quiet moments at the beginning of each day had become precious to her.

She breathed deeply, filling her lungs with the crisp desert air, so clean and fresh and unpolluted it seemed a privilege to be able to breathe it. It was at times like this that she wondered if she could, perhaps, stop her wandering. If she could settle in a place of beauty and let beauty complete the healing process...

Kam had walked ahead, then had apparently realised he no longer had a companion and had turned back towards her.

'Are you coming?' he asked, breaking into her silent communion with the morning.

She hurried towards him, hoping he wouldn't ask what had kept her—she'd feel stupid explaining how she felt.

The little boys she knew joined them, appearing, as always, from nowhere. They greeted her by name and held her hands and danced around her, happy, trusting children whose lives had been ripped apart by war but who had adapted with the resilience of childhood to a different life where fun and happiness were still possible as they played with their friends.

Kam was talking to them, perhaps asking them to guard his car, and they listened and chattered to him, abandoning her now for the far more important male.

'I think you've got it sorted,' she said to Kam as he opened the door of the dusty vehicle then nodded to her to show the radio was still there. 'After you've radioed, a couple of the boys will be happy to show you around the camp—in fact, they'll probably fight for the privilege. I'll get back to the clinic.'

She turned away but heard something in his words 'I'll see you later?' that made her swing back to face him.

Not desperation but some emotion—not the usual casual, offhand remark.

Or was she reading too much into it—was she letting memories of the kiss affect her thinking?

'Hard to avoid it,' she said lightly, 'when we share a patient.'

Returning to the clinic tent, she was surprised to find only Lia in attendance on her husband, who was lying on his side, so his face was turned away from his wife. Thinking Akbar must be sleeping, Jen intended slipping quietly past him, heading for the corner where people were already lining up to have their TB tests or get their medication.

But even in the dim light in this 'hospital' corner, she picked up the sheen of tears on Lia's face. Angry with herself for not knowing the language, she hurried to the testing area and took Aisha to one side.

'Lia is crying—do you know what's wrong? Are Akbar's friends not willing to sit with him? Visit him?'

Aisha's dark eyes glanced towards the rug that separated off the area where Akbar lay.

'He doesn't want his friends, he wants to die,' she said quietly, virtually repeating what Kam had told her during the night, although she'd put Akbar's outburst during the night down to his pain and possibly the effects of the drugs. 'He is angry with his wife, and with the men who carried him back here—probably with you and the other doctor as well. He should be dead, he says.'

'He said this to you?' Jen asked, unable to believe Akbar still felt that way.

'No, he yelled it at his wife when you and the other doctor

went to breakfast. He yelled and yelled, told her not to bring his friends, he had no friends. He told her to let him die.'

Jen knew that cultural differences often created far wider chasms between nationalities than language difficulties.

'Do you understand this?' she asked Aisha.

She first shook her head, then answered with a rather vague, 'Maybe.'

'Maybe?' Jen prompted gently, guessing that Aisha might be embarrassed talking about the reason for Akbar's behaviour.

'Maybe he feels shamed that he didn't save his son. Maybe his—his value as a man is diminished by this failure, and he would not want to live that way.'

Aisha's dark eyes looked pleadingly into Jen's, as if the other woman was begging her to understand the situation without the need for more words.

Jen nodded her response to those pleading eyes. She thought she understood—at least some of it. The man was the strength of the family in this land, the guardian and protector, so it would be natural for Akbar to feel diminished by the loss of his son, and even more devastated by failing to get the boy back.

'We have to get him back,' she said, and Aisha frowned at her.

'Akbar?' she said.

'No, the boy. Hamid. We have to get him back. Surely there's some way—someone we could talk to who has contact with the tribes across the border. Do you know anyone?'

Aisha shook her head, while the shocked look on her pale face suggested she didn't want to know—not anyone or anything—about such a crazy scheme.

Not that Jen was so easily put off.

'Kam knows people in the city,' she said. 'Maybe he will know someone who can intercede for us.'

'Maybe,' Aisha said, repeating a word already used too often in this conversation, although this time when she said it, it was full of doubt.

But as Jen worked through the day, her determination to do something about getting the boy back grew, so when she met up with Kam much later, as she walked towards the rock where she went to watch the sun set over the desert, she couldn't help but bring up the subject.

'If you know people who can drill a well for water, surely you know people who could negotiate for the return of the Akbar's son,' she said, plunging straight into the subject that had been on her mind without a greeting or enquiry about his day. 'Akbar just lies there. His condition isn't critical, and the pain must be easing, yet he has no will to live. In fact, he looks very much as if he's trying to will himself to die.'

Kam studied her for a moment, then waved towards the setting sun.

'Doesn't this beauty steal all other thoughts from your head?' he asked.

Jen looked towards the west, where vermillion and lilac stripes shot through the orange glow.

'Usually it does,' she admitted. 'It's why I come here at this time. But seeing Akbar as he is, seeing Lia's grief at his condition, I can't help but think there has to be something someone can do. Surely a man's life takes precedence over sunsets.'

Kam came towards her and took her hand, leading her onto the flat rock then exerting gentle pressure as he said, 'Sit.'

Jen sat, as much to escape the touch of his hand as from obedience. Memories of their kiss fluttered uneasily in her body, and she clung desperately to thoughts of Akbar and the grieving Lia to keep those memories at bay.

'Now, breathe in the cooling night air and watch the sunset,' Kam ordered. 'Akbar isn't going to die in the next ten minutes, or even the next half-hour. Maybe when the beauty of the desert creeps into your soul, it will ease a little of the anguish you are feeling for the couple.'

I don't want the beauty of the desert creeping in, she wanted to say. It is too seductive, too all-encompassing.

Too romantic!

There, it was said, if only in her head, but it worried her that she'd sat here every night since she'd come to the camp and enjoyed the beauty without a thought of romance, although she'd often thought of David and wondered what he would think of the nomadic life she led now, so far removed from the house in the suburbs and the little family that they'd planned.

The Jenny whom David had known had been a very different person, not better, or less good, just different...

'You are still thinking of Akbar.'

Kam's accusation broke into her thoughts and she turned towards him, wondering why he thought that.

'Actually, I'm not,' she said, and thought that would be the end of it but, no, he was apparently a persistent man.

'Then why the frown?' he asked. 'A sunset cannot make you frown.'

Jen put her hands up and wiped them across her face, hoping to clear it of all expression.

She must have failed for his quiet 'Tell me,' was a command and suddenly Jen knew she would.

'I lost my husband in the accident I had, my husband and my unborn son. This agony of Akbar's brings it back, although his son is still alive...'

She felt him move so his arm drew her closer, easing them both into the shadow of the rock.

'Is this why you travel? Why you can't stay still?' He had slid her scarf back off her hair and was dropping kisses on the top of her head. 'Is it the pain of loss that keeps you moving?'

The kisses were more of a problem than the questions. In fact, the questions were easily answered.

'The pain goes away, you know,' she managed, 'in time. You don't forget but it doesn't hurt each time you breathe. Then it doesn't hurt when you look at happy couples, and finally you can hold a child in your arms and while there's a hollow deep inside, it's not an ache.'

How could such quiet words hurt *him* so badly? Kam wondered, tightening his arms around the woman while emotion squeezed his heart. It seemed natural to kiss her, to move his lips from hair, to cheek, to chin and then to lips, and if her fierce response was born in memory, at least he knew enough to tell she was responding to him, not to a ghost from the past.

His was the name that trembled on her lips as he lifted his head the better to see her face in the dusk light, his the name she whispered as she leaned into him and raised her mouth to his again.

He captured it, that mouth, with its lush lips, and explored its depth and hunger, marvelling that life should so unexpectedly provide him with such a sweet surprise. All thought of the work he had to do, the wrongs he had to put right, were washed from his mind by fascination and desire.

The kiss they shared was different to anything she'd ever experienced, Jen realised as she drew in a deep breath to replenish the air Kam had stolen. It was as elemental as the night and the desert that lay before them, man and woman giving and receiving pleasure, although the heat building inside her suggested kisses would soon not be enough for either of them, and with prayers finished she could hear people moving around the camp, quiet voices calling to each other.

She dragged herself out of Kam's strong embrace, putting a little space between them.

'We were talking about work,' she reminded him. 'About Akbar…'

Kam released her, but she thought his hands moved reluctantly off her shoulders.

'We were talking about you,' he reminded her, his voice so husky she wondered if he'd been as deeply affected by the kisses as she had.

Not that she could admit it…

She shook her head.

'Before that,' she reminded him. 'Akbar, our patient, and Hamid, his son.'

Kam turned away from her and she heard a deep sigh.

'OK, but I refuse to discuss it out here. Later, in the tent— in the hospital if we can think of it that way—there we will talk. For a start you do not know who has the child, which of the warring tribes. This isn't something you can go into—is the expression half-cocked?'

Jen nodded absently, more or less agreeing with what he was saying but thinking more that the beauty of the sunset *was* seeping into her soul and working the magic it usually worked, relieving the tensions of the day—the tensions of the kiss—and reminding her of all that was good and beautiful in the world.

She leaned back against the rock she considered her personal back-rest and stretched her legs out in front of her, relaxing as the dusk crept in, turning the desert sands from vivid orange to pink and blue and purple.

'Such a beautiful place,' she murmured, but even as she said it, some echo of Kam's conversation rattled in her head. *Is the expression half-cocked?* he'd asked. Why? Was it an Australian expression, not an English one?

Not that he'd said he was English, had he?

The suspicions she'd harboured the previous day about Kam being a spy had sneaked beneath her defences, worse now because she'd kissed him. But though she studied him in the dimming light, she didn't mention these sudden and disturbing doubts, asking instead about his day and what he'd seen.

'The boys took me everywhere,' he said, and maybe because of her reawakening suspicion she began to worry whether taking him 'everywhere' in the camp had been such a good idea. What if he *was* a spy, not for the government or Aid for All, but for one of the warring factions? What if he was checking out the camp to see the best way to attack it?

And she'd been kissing him!

Forget kissing. What if she'd put the refugees at risk by being so obliging to him?

The questions made her queasy, and she shifted against the rock. There was one way to find out, but would he tell the truth?

'Are you really working for Aid for All?' she asked, when the queasiness threatened to overcome her.

'Why wouldn't I be?' he parried, which increased both suspicion and queasiness a hundredfold.

'That's not an answer,' Jen snapped, remembering the kiss again. Had she kissed a traitor?

'But who else would I be working for?' he asked, still avoiding a straightforward yes or no.

'The government, the warring tribes, who knows? You could be a spy—even working for Aid for All you could be spying on me, Aisha and Marij, reporting back to someone. I don't know. It just seems strange that after all these months someone appears out of the blue to offer help and wells and clinics. You might be promising these things to distract us from what you're really doing here—how would we know?'

Kam stood up then reached out his hand, silently offering to help her to her feet.

'You have to trust,' he said, and she wasn't sure whether he meant trust in taking his hand or in believing him.

She didn't take his hand just in case, although that was more to do with the dangers of touching him than trust.

'I'll stay a little longer,' she said.

What had he said or done to make her so suspicious? Kam wondered as he made his way towards the clinic tent, intending to check on Akbar before going for his dinner. People were moving about the camp in the dusk, gowned figures flitting here and there, and he realised how easy it would be for the warring tribes to have spies here.

Though spying on what? What more could be taken from these poor, stateless people?

'I am here to see how things are running and what the needs are,' he told Jenny, meeting up with her later in the food tent. 'From both a government angle and as far as Aid for All is concerned. I'm here to see what's being done and what more needs to be done.'

He spoke flatly. The idea that she might not trust him had upset him more than it should have, and Akbar's condition made things worse as the man refused to speak to anyone, refused to eat or drink, and when he had felt strong enough to sit up, he'd begun picking out the stitches on his chest and legs, cutting through the sutures with a rusty razor-blade a friend must have provided for him. Kam had considered taking the razor blade off him, but knew Akbar would then tear the stitches out and create far worse wounds.

Did Jenny know this that she was so intent on getting the boy back?

He didn't like to ask in case she didn't know—finding out would make her more upset.

So he sat and ate, waiting to see if she would respond to his explanation or perhaps tell him why she doubted him.

'So, I know you would only get a very general idea of how things are from one walk through the camp, but what did you find today?'

Was she testing him?

Kam couldn't tell, for her head was bent and her face in shadow.

'Jenny.' He said her name, but quietly, then waited until she did look up, her eyes dark in the shadowy tent, the pale oval of her face framed by the dark scarf. 'You can trust me,' he said, 'in every way. The fate of these people as well as their comfort and health and welfare is as important to me as it is to you. Do you believe me?'

She studied him, tilting her head to one side as if that might give her a different perspective, but it was his motives, not his looks, she had to be considering.

'I would like to,' she said, 'because these people are so vulnerable.'

She put down her dish and held out her hands in a helpless kind of gesture.

'And even if you are some kind of spy, what can I do? I can ask you to have compassion in your heart. To see their plight and maybe report on it, but not make things worse for them. I could beg, I suppose, trade kisses that would have no meaning, but in the end it is between you and your conscience what you do.'

The trade-kisses part made Kam's heart race, but only until he realised just how demeaning a suggestion it had been, especially coming after the kisses they'd shared not long ago—kisses of passion and desire, he'd thought.

But he'd asked for it, daring her to trade a kiss last night, but now he hurt for her that she felt such doubt, yet he couldn't make things right.

Not yet!

Except as far as kisses went. He could sort that out.

'Your kisses are too valuable for any currency but love,' he said. 'What we shared this evening grew from attraction and perhaps a little from pain. I doubt you can deny the attraction, Jenny, and I certainly can't. But…'

She half smiled at him.

'There's always a but, isn't there?' she said, so much sadness and regret in her voice he wanted to hold her again—kiss her again.

Instead, he nodded.

'Yes, there's always a but,' he agreed. 'Another time, another place, we might have met and kissed and enjoyed the attraction that has sparked between us, but suspicion is a bad basis for such things, and right now my life is bounded by demands I can't explain. Right now, seizing the moment and enjoying the attraction would be all that could happen between us, and I doubt that, even without the suspicion, you would enjoy such a relationship.'

Jen sighed as the words ran through her mind, then ran through again—poetic words, and things he couldn't explain.

'So I remain suspicious and kisses are forbidden,' she said, speaking quietly, half-teasing, although the other half was sadness.

Then Kam smiled and she felt the flare of heat again.

'Oh, I don't know that we can't kiss again,' he murmured. 'As long as we both understand that's all they are. Just kisses, not currency, or promises…'

Just kisses?

The flare of heat spread through Jenny's body, sending tingling messages along her nerves.

Would it hurt?

Harm anyone?

'Just kisses?' she repeated, and saw him glance at his watch.

'We should check Akbar first, then perhaps a walk along the edge of the plateau? The moon should be full enough to light our way.'

The tingling messages turned to shivers of apprehension, but Jen knew she'd nod agreement. That she could still feel longing and desire had been a revelation, like a rebirth almost, so surely it would do no harm to see where such a rebirth would lead.

Where moonlit kisses would lead…

CHAPTER SIX

THEY walked back to the clinic tent together, saying nothing more about the proposed meeting, although to Jen the anticipation seemed to spark in the air around them.

Kam knelt by Akbar, who appeared to be sleeping, perhaps trying to persuade Lia to get some sleep as well. Jen went on into her private corner, thankful she'd got through all the slides and medication lists during the day so there was no work awaiting her.

She wanted desperately to wash and change into something prettier than jeans and shirt and a long grey tunic. But that would look stupid, as if she was going on a date…

Changing clothes would look stupid?

What on earth was she thinking?

What could be more stupid than walking in the moonlight and trading kisses with a man who'd already said quite clearly he wasn't interested in her? A man who hadn't denied he might be a spy? Was she nuts? Of course she couldn't do it!

She undid her braid and brushed her hair before pinning it into a loose knot on top of her head and was about to strip off her working clothes when a commotion outside led her back into the main part of the tent.

Three of the small boys she knew were standing in the doorway next to a man in a black robe so old the fabric looked rusty. He had a black scarf rolled into a rope and wound around his head so only his eyes and his lips were visible.

He spoke and Kam moved so swiftly, grabbing the man's arm and hurrying him further out of the tent, that Jen felt a flash of fear. Was the man a messenger for Kam? Did this prove he *was* a spy?

Jen followed—after all, this was *her* clinic, not his.

As she came out of the tent the man gesticulated towards her and spoke again, Kam slamming words at him, obviously not agreeing, but the man kept pointing at Jenny.

'Go back inside,' Kam ordered, sounding so furious Jen almost obeyed, but somehow she was caught up in this, and, with the unease of distrust between them, she wasn't going anywhere.

'What are they saying?' she asked the boys, wide-eyed on-lookers to the confrontation. She knew they didn't speak much English but they were picking up more each day.

'That man wants you to go with him to the chief because chief's wife having baby.'

The child who had explained this pointed to the stranger.

'Go where? What chief?' Jen asked, and Kam shot some kind of command at the boys which not only silenced them but made them step back into the shadows.

'Then *you* tell me what's happening,' Jen demanded of Kam. 'And tell me the truth—no lies or evasions, thank you!'

He looked at her and shook his head.

'You should have stayed inside,' he muttered, and she threw him a furious glare which he obviously understood because he then explained.

'The wife of the leader of one of the warring tribes, the one who has taken over the village where most of the refugees lived, has been in labour eighteen hours. The woman who acts as midwife has told the chief the baby won't come out. He wants you there to help. I imagine he knows about Caesareans and assumes you can do one. I have been trying to tell him I can do one, but he—'

'The chief doesn't want a man touching his wife,' Jen finished for him.

Kam gave a grim nod, though he did add, 'And if you hadn't come out of the tent I could have told him you were away and I'd have to go.'

'What nonsense,' Jen said. 'These people aren't barbarians.'

Images of Akbar's flayed and battered body flashed before her eyes, and after them images of Akbar's acute distress.

'But it's perfect,' Jen said, suddenly excited. 'Tell him I'll come but only on condition we bring back Akbar's son as payment.'

'You can't make conditions with these people,' Kam protested. 'You don't even know if you'll come back yourself.'

'If we make a pact they'll honour it—I've been here long enough to know that honour exists among the tribes. Once someone's word is given, it is kept.'

Kam gave her one last frown then turned and spoke to the messenger, whose dark eyes flashed between Kam and Jenny as Kam was speaking.

'I'll pack a bag with what I might need,' Jenny said, and slipped inside the tent, stopping beside Lia to ask if she had a photo of Hamid. Lia's English wasn't good but eventually she reached into the folds of her gown and produced a small picture of a little boy, then a picture of the three of them, parents and child, both pictures worn and grey, as if looking at them had drained them of their shininess.

Jen slipped them both into her bag, found a warm scarf to wrap around her head and shoulders. Would they be walking or driving? Please, don't let it be riding on a camel—she found the favoured beasts unstable to say the least.

Outside, Kam and the stranger were still arguing, and as she appeared the stranger stepped forward and grabbed her arm, using one English word. 'Come.'

Jen pulled away from him, taking a step backwards, although she knew she couldn't waste too much time as the lives of both the mother and the unborn infant could be in danger.

'Has he agreed?' she asked Kam, who shook his head.

Time for bluff.

'Then I don't go!' she said, and turned to walk back inside the tent.

'Come!' the man repeated, but it wasn't the order made her turn but Kam's quick gasp.

The man had produced a long and very dangerous-looking rifle from beneath his robes and was now pointing it at her.

She took a deep breath and remained right where she was, staring defiantly into the dark slit where his eyes were.

'Tell him if he shoots me, the woman and the child will die and his leader will be very angry with him.'

Kam said something, and Jen had to assume he was translating what she'd said. Slowly the stranger lowered the rifle until it was pointing at the ground.

Kam spoke to him again, and this time he nodded.

'OK,' Kam said, grabbing Jenny almost roughly by the arm, 'you've got your agreement, although that was the most damn stupid thing I've ever seen anyone do. What if he'd shot you?'

She turned and smiled at him, although the smile was to hide the fact her lips were probably trembling—every other bit of her was. She'd never been so terrified in her life but she'd known she had to hide it—to show strength and determination in front of the man with the gun.

Kam walked with her as she followed the dark-gowned figure through the camp, aware of whispering as they passed and hisses of fear or disgust rising into the night air.

'If I'm not back tomorrow, you'll have to carry on the testing,' she said to Kam. 'The girls know the system, it's just the slides you have to check and compare to the others.'

'If you're not back tomorrow, I won't be either,' he said. 'Surely you didn't think I'd let you go alone?'

She wanted to stop right there and argue with him, but the black-robed man was striding on ahead and she wasn't sure just how badly off the pregnant woman might be, so she kept walking, berating Kam as she went.

'You can't come with me—that's just stupid. What happens if they keep us both—what will happen to the clinic with no doctor? Besides, I thought the man said he didn't want you.'

'He didn't want me as a doctor but I told him you don't speak the language and I would need to be there to explain to the chief exactly what was happening with his wife. I did rather emphasise the fact that the chief would be extremely worried if he didn't know what was going on and if you couldn't ask him for permission to do an operation. I added a bit of medical drama to make a Caesar seem a bit worse than it is, and our friend up ahead was probably turning green under his turban and decided better me than him telling that kind of stuff to the chief.'

'It's still stupid!' Jen muttered, not willing to admit she felt far braver about this adventure now she knew Kam was coming, although a little sick in her stomach when she thought of something happening to him.

These were the people who had beaten up Akbar.

They had reached the outer limits of the camp and to her relief she saw a battered vehicle standing beyond the loose wire boundary. No camels!

'Make sure he understands we want safe passage back here and we want the boy,' Jen said to Kam before agreeing to climb in.

Kam spoke and the man held up his hand as if giving some kind of oath then hustled them both into the car and took off, speeding through the moonlit night. If they were on a road, it wasn't discernible to Jen, but she was in the back seat so maybe Kam could see it from the front. Not that the man seemed to need a road. The vehicle was twisting and turning around the dunes, heading around the base of the mountains before beginning to climb.

'I know this place,' Kam said. 'As a child I was sometimes brought here to these mountains. I think there's a way across them back to our camp, a track Akbar probably took, maybe ten miles long, from memory.'

The driver said something to him, the voice indicative of an order, and Kam shrugged his shoulders but stopped talking.

Ten miles wasn't far to walk, Jen decided, if they had to make their own way back to the camp. Though over the mountains? From the camp side the mountains looked steep and not at all user-friendly, but if there was a track…

An hour into their journey the driver slowed, and ahead Jenny could see lights.

So this was the village where most of their refugees had

lived. The houses up ahead had been their homes, the gentle mountain slopes their grazing land. By moonlight it was a pretty place, the houses built of stone or mortar mixed from sand hard up against the cliffs.

But there were tents here, too, the black Bedouin tents she now knew so well, and it was outside one of these their driver stopped.

Fear caught at Jenny's throat and she breathed deeply. For all they were at war and had driven the refugees out, she reminded herself, they were honourable people in their own way.

Their guide barked an order at Kam, who got out and opened the back door for Jenny, giving her shoulder a little squeeze and keeping close to her as they moved towards the open doorway of the big tent. That hand on her shoulder and the closeness of his body rebuilt her strength, and she wondered that she could feel such trust in a man she'd doubted.

But at the doorway another man held up his hand, barring Kam's way and speaking so quickly Jen knew Kam's knowledge of the language must be good for him to follow it.

'This is the women's tent,' he said to Jenny, this time taking her hand while he spoke. Guessing she was fearful and in need of support? 'Our friend and I will not be allowed in, but the chief is just outside around the back. We will go and talk to him, then I will talk to you through the walls. You'll be all right?'

He squeezed her fingers gently and his eyes scanned her face, but she couldn't let him know how apprehensive she was feeling. She nodded, then, hearing a cry of pain from within, quickly broke away, although she turned back at the last moment, fishing the two photos from her pocket.

'Hamid,' she said. 'Make them give you Hamid. He must be with you or I won't help the woman.'

Jen knew she was bluffing, and she was reasonably sure that Kam also knew she was bluffing, but would the chief know?

That was the risk they had to take.

A woman took Jenny's hand and led her deep into the tent, where a lamp lit up a scene that could have been repeated in tents all over the Arabian Peninsula down through thousands of years. A young woman, bundled in clothes, lay on a pile of mats and a palliasse in the middle of the tent, other women kneeling and sitting cross-legged around her, one bathing her face, others holding her hands, all of them talking in their sing-song voices very quietly and, Jen guessed, encouragingly.

The girl herself—and she was only a girl—was extraordinarily attractive, even though her face was grey with fatigue and almost black circles lay beneath her huge dark eyes.

And those eyes held fear—Jen could see it. She knelt beside the girl and took her hands, talking to her, saying words she wouldn't understand but hoping her tone might convey reassurance.

'I'm going to examine her now. I'd like to remove some of the clothes she's wearing so I can palpate her abdomen at the next contraction and I'd like someone to tell me exactly what's happened so far.'

Jen spoke loudly, hoping Kam was outside the right part of the tent, then she heard his voice, talking quietly but quite audibly, and one of the women, talking all the time, began to pull the blankets off the girl, finally revealing her swollen belly.

'The woman says the contractions grew weaker and weaker. She is obviously an experienced midwife and she says she could poke her finger quite deeply into the

patient's belly during a contraction at the end,' Kam translated, while the woman who had spoken demonstrated this
for Jenny then held her fingers apart to show how far the
cervix had dilated.

'I'm going to listen to the foetal heartbeat. I'll make do
with my stethoscope,' she said to Kam, who immediately
translated. Jenny was strengthened by his voice and by his
presence not far away. She went to work more steadily now,
letting her training take over.

'The FHR is slow, under a hundred. I would have thought
tachycardia would be indicative of a problem, but the brady-
cardia is a worry anyway if it goes on for more than ten
minutes. I'll check again later. Can you ask how long since
she had a contraction?'

The patient was getting agitated and the women had to hold
her shoulders down until Jen gently pushed them away and
helped the girl sit up. She cursed herself for not knowing the
language but she kept her arm around the girl and patted her
shoulder, smoothing back the sweaty, tangled hair from her
exhausted face.

'No contraction for half an hour and before that very weak,'
Kam said. 'Is the patient all right? Is that her crying out?'

'Yes. What's she saying? What does she want?'

'She wants her husband,' Kam translated, his voice
sounding very dubious.

'What's the man's name?' Jen demanded.

'Abdullah.'

Jen repeated it and her patient grabbed her hands and
looked pleadingly into Jen's face, repeating the name and
pointing to herself.

'Why can't he come in?' Jen asked Kam.

The answer was brief.

'Custom!'

'Oh, spare me,' Jen said. 'You tell him he's a modern man, a leader, and it's up to him to start and set new customs for his people. What sort of leader is he that he bows to ancient ways at a time like this? OK, some of them are good, but others must be tossed out. Say it any way you like, but tell that man to get his butt in here to reassure this poor woman. He needn't stay—in fact, I doubt he'd be much help during a Caesar—but she's so distressed she needs to see him and she needs to see him now.'

While Kam's voice rose and fell outside, Jen finished her examination. The contractions must have lost force early in the latent phase for the cervix hadn't reached four centimetres dilatation. After twenty hours this poor young girl was still in the first stage of labour.

Jen's admittedly basic physical examination suggested it was a problem with the girl's pelvis, the bones failing to open wide enough to allow the baby's descent.

Then voices at the doorway and a flutter of rearranging of scarves among the women suggested Kam might have persuaded the chief to enter the tent to see his wife.

Jen rearranged the rugs and clothing over the girl's belly and again pushed her limp hair back from her face.

A deep voice spoke and the women scattered like pigeons in a square, then a huge man appeared.

'I have got my butt in here!' he said, in a deep, guttural voice, and Jenny had to smile.

'How long would you have gone on letting my colleague translate?' she asked as he strode towards them, his eyes on his young wife on the bed.

'Perhaps for the whole time,' he said, 'for why would you believe you needed someone to translate?'

He knelt beside the bed and began to speak very gently to his wife, and once again the language sounded like poetry.

Jen let the two of them talk for a few minutes then she knelt on the other side.

'I brought my colleague in case you wouldn't come in, then he would have had to explain to your wife what we need to do. The labour has gone on too long. I think perhaps because your wife's pelvis won't allow the baby through.'

She pointed to her own pelvic region and used her hands to show how the pelvic bones usually opened.

'I think the baby is now getting distressed, and as you can see, your wife is exhausted. I would like to do a Caesarean and deliver the baby that way. You know what it means?'

'You cut her open and take out the baby. Will she live, my wife?'

Jen could have hugged him. So often people thought first of the child—would it live?—but this man must dearly love his wife for her to be the most important issue in his mind.

'She will, but she will have to take it easy for a few days— she should move her legs and walk a little but not move around too much or strain herself, just until the scars, both internal and external, heal. I can come back and see her every day if you wish.'

The man nodded then began to speak to his wife, who looked at him with her lovely eyes brimming tears, while her two hands clung to one of his.

He shook his head, and though Jen knew Kam could probably hear the conversation, he knew better than to interrupt whatever was passing between the two of them.

'She wants me to stay,' the big man said, looking pale himself now, as if he'd rather be facing a thousand fighting tribesmen than be present at his baby's birth.

'Men do it all the time in the West,' she told him. 'Even with a Caesarean birth. We can hang up a rug so you can sit at your wife's head and not have to see the operation. I will give her an anaesthetic so she won't know you're there, but I know you will honour your word. And if you are there, we can hand the newborn baby to you, and you can cut the umbilical cord if you wish, so you are part of this great occasion and will be the first to hold your child.'

The man took a deep breath, looked down at his pale child bride and nodded.

'I will do it,' he said, and began to give orders so the women came scurrying back, and in no time there was a rug hung above the woman's waist.

'I need my colleague to assist me,' Jen told the leader. 'It will be easier and safer if he is here. He can remain behind the rug with you, giving your wife the anaesthetic and oxygen to ensure she and the baby are all right. I will also need water and some clean cloth and something to wrap the baby in when it is born.'

More orders, then Kam appeared in the doorway. He took in the situation in a glance and made his way to the head of the makeshift bed and knelt on the other side of patient's head.

'I'm doing the anaesthetic?'

A smile for Jenny's benefit. She was thankful for it, aware her heart was racing with what ifs.

What if she botched the operation and the baby died?

The woman died?

'It's ether—you can use it?' Jen said, handing him a bottle

and a swab to pour some drops onto. 'She might feel nauseous after this anaesthetic,' she explained to the chief, 'but it is all we have.'

Jen rummaged around in her bag and produced the small canister of oxygen she'd dug up from a corner of her room and passed this with a mask and tubing to Kam. She set out the instruments she'd need—scalpel, retractors and small clamps being the most important. She didn't have any obstetric forceps but felt she could manage with her hands, although that might mean her patient would have a larger scar than was strictly necessary.

All these things rattled around in her head as she mentally rehearsed what she was about to do. Then, as a woman put down a basin of water and a pile of spotless-looking cloths beside her, Jen washed and soaped her hands, dried them and pulled on gloves.

The woman Jen had taken to be the midwife remained beside her and Jen was glad she had someone on hand to take the baby and see to it while she finished the operation.

'Ready,' she said to Kam.

'I'll tell you when,' he said, and although she couldn't see him, she knew he'd be pressing the ether-sprinkled pad to the patient's nose and counting slowly down.

'Ready,' he said, and Jen began, swabbing then cutting through the skin and outer flesh through the uterine wall, keeping the incisions as small as possible, feeling for the baby's head then gently easing him out—for it was a him.

'You have a fine son,' she said, handing it to the waiting woman, who used a tiny straw to suction out his nose and mouth. 'In a minute, when we know he's breathing real air and turning pink, you can hold him. Do you want to cut the cord?'

A strangled 'No' was the answer, so Jen cut and knotted it then motioned to the woman to pass the baby to his father.

The woman hung back so Jen took the baby, now a satisfactory pink, his eyes wide open as if to take in all he could of this new world. She held him close for a moment and thought of all that might have been, but the past was gone and with it other dreams and plans and happiness. This was now, and a new life was just beginning. She dropped a kiss on the cloth swaddled around the little head, then leaned around the rug to hand him to the man who sat there, still holding his wife's unresponsive hand.

Keeping his promise.

An honourable man.

He took the tiny child, a look of wonder akin to disbelief on his bearded face and tears in his dark eyes, but though he held the child, he turned his attention back to his unconscious wife. The deep love he felt for her was almost palpable.

Jen delivered the placenta and sewed up the wounds she'd made, checking for any signs of bleeding as she went.

'I'm putting a dressing on her now,' Jen said to Kam, knowing he would be watching the woman's eyes for signs of returning consciousness. 'Let's see how clever you were at judging dosage.'

'If you knew how long it was since I used ether,' he grumbled. 'In fact, I don't know that I've ever used it.'

'Everyone can use it,' Jen reminded him. 'Didn't dentists use it for a long time in the past?'

'She's coming round,' Kam said, and his voice told her how relieved he was. 'Have you any pain relief we can give her? The wound will hurt like hell.'

'She will forget her pain when she sees her son,' the chief said, but Jen wasn't so sure.

'I've got some tablets I will leave for her,' Jen said, speaking to the chief again. 'Do you have access to ice, or is that a stupid question?'

'We have power in the village and refrigerators. I can get ice,' he said, so Jen explained how wrapping ice in towels and holding it against the stomach might help reduce the pain.

'And make her take the painkillers—she can still breast-feed her baby without them affecting her milk.'

One look at Kam's face was enough to tell her that this was not the kind of conversation this desert chief was used to, but the man was holding up very well, mainly because most of his attention was back on the tiny being in his arms, who was wriggling now and then and gazing up at his bearded father as if taking in every detail of the man who held him.

The patient stirred and groaned, and Jenny wondered if she should give her something stronger than an oral analgesic until the maltreated parts of her body settled down, but then her husband bent towards her, tilting the baby so she could see his face, and wonder overtook the pain.

She reached out a tentative finger and touched a tightly clenched fist, then she looked up at her husband, the question—is he really ours?—obvious in her eyes.

Kam slipped away and Jen roughly washed her instruments, wrapped them in a clean cloth so she could take them home to sterilise them and moved towards the door, leaving the pair to examine their miracle together.

'Have you asked about Hamid?' she asked, joining Kam outside the doorway.

'They will get him when we are ready to leave,' Kam said, but something in his voice made her turn and look into his face.

'You don't believe him?'

'Oh, I believe him, it's the "when we are ready to leave" part that bothers me,' he said. 'Do you think that man will let you go when his wife still needs care? Do you know what it would have taken for a man like him to be present at the birth of his child? He is going against thousands of years of tradition, which tells me he must love her very, very much. Do you think he's not going to worry about her recovery? Not want a trained person taking care of her?'

'But I can't stay,' Jen protested. 'And he promised.'

Kam touched her arm, no doubt to calm her, although she was feeling far from calm.

'It wasn't he who promised,' Kam reminded her, 'but his lieutenant. Desert people are very wary about making promises because their word is their bond. So they will avoid giving it. They will procrastinate as long as possible or seek an out. In this man's case, the out is his lieutenant. He's the one who gave his word.'

'Well, it was that or shoot me, I suppose,' Jen said, and although she spoke lightly, she was feeling a great deal of disquiet.

'Don't worry,' Kam said. 'I'll find the man who promised and talk to him. He is obviously trusted by his chief that he was sent on the mission, so he must be important to the tribe. What if you write out exactly what must be done for your patient—when to give her painkillers and how many, when to check the dressing and change it if necessary? Have you enough dressings and antiseptic to leave some for them? I'll check the chief reads English as well as he speaks it and if not will translate your instructions. We'll set everything up then tell them we can come back—when? A week?'

Jenny thought about it, her imagination providing lists of things that could go wrong for the young mother.

'I don't know, Kam,' she finally said, and must have sounded so despairing he put his arm around her and gave her a hug. She nestled gratefully against him, drawing strength from his body. 'Not a week certainly. Imagine if infection set in!'

Comforting, that's what it was, to have his arm around her shoulders, and if it started little tremors of desire at the same time—well, she didn't have to acknowledge that part.

What she had to do was concentrate on the problem.

'It didn't take us that long to get here. What if we take Hamid back tonight and I promise to come over again each night to check on her?'

Kam gave a long, theatrical sigh.

'So much for kissing in the moonlight,' he said, squeezing her a little closer.

'That was never going to happen,' Jenny told him. 'I'd come to my senses just before the messenger arrived. As you said, this can go nowhere, so why…?'

She shrugged away the rest of the explanation and eased away from him before he felt the tremors in her body. Only this time they weren't just tremors of desire, they were tremors of disappointment as well.

But Kam must have felt something, for he moved away as quickly as if she'd pushed him.

'I'll find our guide,' he said, and disappeared into the shadows.

CHAPTER SEVEN

THE guide returned but his face was grim. He spoke to Kam, and now it was his turn to look grim.

And angry!

'Apparently the chief says we cannot go,' he translated, but something in his tone told Jen that wasn't right.

Although it wasn't hard to guess what bothered him.

'*We* cannot go?' she repeated, with just enough emphasis on the first word for him to understand she'd guessed the things he hadn't said.

'The chief wants you to stay. I have offered, and explained I can do whatever is necessary for the woman should things change. I said I could work through the midwife here, but the chief wants you.'

'And Hamid?'

'Our guide says Hamid is waiting for us—he has him safe.'

'Then you could take Hamid back and run the testing for a while. The two nurses know what to do—all you'd have to do is check the slides and put out the medication. I'll stay for another day and—'

Kam couldn't believe she'd be stupid enough to suggest such a thing, and his anger at her, and at the situation, made his abrupt 'No!' sound far too loud, too aggressive, too explosive.

'One goes, we all go,' he insisted. 'You've said you'll return. Why should your word be any less believable than theirs?'

Useless question. He knew why. For centuries these people—his people—had trusted no one but their own, often with good reason as waves of raiders and conquerors had swept across their lands.

He spoke to their guide, who was adamant Jenny could not leave the camp, although he seemed shamed to have to say that.

'Well, she needs to sleep. At least show us to somewhere we can sleep, and we want the boy with us—that was your promise.'

Their guide nodded and led the way to a small cave, hollowed out over the centuries by the nomads as shelter and home during their summer stays in the mountains. Inside, lit by the dim light of a tallow lamp, the little boy already lay asleep, the photos clutched tightly in his hands.

Jenny squatted beside him and watched him as he slept, then she looked up at Kam and smiled.

'So we've saved two children today,' she said softly, and in the words he heard an echo of the child she hadn't saved. That she could be so—so brave—about this situation affected him deeply, sparking anger deep inside.

'Saved him? Don't you realise the situation? We're far from saved, and neither is Hamid, and now we're at the mercy of the chief.'

Jen shook her head.

'Do you really believe he'll harm us?' she said, and Kam couldn't tell a lie.

'No, not harm us, but he could keep us here indefinitely.'

'Not us—me,' Jen argued. 'You can go, the guide will take

you back, you and Hamid, which will stop Akbar's self-destruction, and it will mean the testing can go on.'

'Forget the testing!' Kam all but yelled the words, remembering the sleeping child and stopping himself just in time. 'And forget about me going back and leaving you here, that is just not going to happen.'

But even as he spoke, he knew he had to do something. For a start, if Arun didn't hear from him for twenty-four hours, he would start to worry. The way the country was, they'd both known that Kam going out into the far reaches of it had been the most dangerous job, for if he was recognised by anyone against the hereditary regime, he could be captured or even killed.

And here, should someone recognise him, he'd make the perfect kidnap victim, held to ransom to finance the struggle going on between the tribes.

They had to get away.

Tonight!

'Did you write out the list of what to do for your patient?' he asked Jen.

'I left it there, but I can tell you what was on it if you want to write it in your language.'

She dug into her bag and brought out a pen and small pad, handing them to Kam then telling him what to write, taking her time as he was translating as he went.

'They must watch for signs of fever—I've left antibiotics for her to take and the chief understands she has to take them regularly until the course is finished, but if she starts to run a temperature, they should give her aspirin as well, and bathe her to keep her cool. When I come back I'll bring more antibiotics, stronger ones, just in case.'

He finished the care instructions then kept writing, the curvy script filling another page. Once done, he set it down on the ground and put a rock on it, with Jen's medical bag beside it, then indicated a pile of mats that would serve as their beds.

'Piled together they'll be softer, but I can split them so we have separate beds,' he suggested, watching Jen's face in the dim light, wondering if she'd dare to lie close to him.

And why was he suggesting it?

He wasn't sure, except he had this urgent need to keep her safe, and if she was wrapped in his arms, that would go some way towards achieving his aim.

Not that he intended sleeping for very long. He was going to get them out of here tonight—all three of them.

'I guess the pile of mats would be more comfortable,' Jen said, but so tentatively he wondered if he should forget the holding-her-in-his-arms idea. He could keep her safe if she slept against the wall of the cave and he slept between her and the door. Although, even in this tense and potentially deadly situation, his arms ached to hold her for other reasons.

'You're not happy about it?' he asked, and watched her face.

A tentative smile hovered around her lips and he was sure she was blushing beneath the golden freckles, although the dim light made it impossible to tell.

'With what we feel—the attraction—is it a good idea...?'

The hesitant phrases dropped so confusedly from her lips it was all he could do not to take her in his arms right then and there, to comfort and protect her. But he didn't want to make the situation more difficult than it already was, and his mind needed to be focussed on escape, not attraction.

'I'm being ridiculous, aren't I?' she said, turning so he could see her face in the lamplight. 'But it's been five years since David died. Five years since I've felt something even close to attraction to another man.' The halting confession faltered, then she lifted her chin and continued. 'It's not that I thought I'd never love again, although I did think that for a long time, but it's as if what we had was so special it couldn't be replicated. Now here I am, stuck in the desert with a very sexy man, feeling all kinds of things I've never felt before, and I'm confused.'

'Why?'

She smiled a real smile this time.

'I suppose because I think you're sexy, for a start. Because I noticed, and because I felt something I didn't expect to feel, and yet it's for a man who has no interest in a relationship, so it's something that has no future, and I honestly don't know that I can handle that kind of thing. With my husband, we met and fell in love and got married. I've had no practice at any other kind of relationship, but I do know when he died it nearly killed me, so I don't want to love like that again—to love and lose someone. Yet if I give in to this attraction and it leads to love, that's exactly what will happen.'

Kam stared at her.

'Is this the woman who travels all over the world, often to very unpleasant places, and exults in the challenge, the adventure, the fun? Can't you see that sexual relationships are all of those things? That they can be part of your life, and make it fuller and more exciting?'

Jen studied him for a moment.

'No, I can't see that. Oh, I know it works for some people. My best friend can handle love affairs but that's because she doesn't want any more than the fun and adventure and challenge as far as her liaisons are concerned. She's married to her career and she looks on a little fling with someone as relaxation. But me? I just know I'd make a mess of it, Kam.'

He reached out and drew her into his arms and held her close against his body.

'No kisses, then, I promise,' he said softly. 'But lie with me. That way I'll know you're safe.'

He led her to the pile of rugs and pushed her shoulders gently so she sat, then he knelt and took off her sandals, his hands warm against her skin, the little act of kindness so unexpectedly intimate Jen felt the desire she was fighting ripple through her once again.

But as she lay down on the pile of mats and Kam settled beside her, she glanced towards the sleeping child, and she wondered if they should draw him in, put him between them, not to keep herself safe from her own emotions but to keep him safe.

'Hamid?' she whispered to Kam.

'I will watch him—he'll be safe.'

'But you need to sleep yourself,' Jen protested, and she felt his arm wrap around her shoulder and draw her closer.

'When both of you are sleeping, I will doze,' he said. 'Now, go to sleep, Jenny Stapleton, before I forget I am here to protect you not make love to you.'

How could she sleep when his arm lay heavy on her shoulders and her body felt his warmth and wanted more of it?

How could she sleep when remembered delights of lovemaking were flickering not only in her body but in her mind?

How could she sleep—?

She'd think of Hamid, the child they'd saved, or would save. Kam had said so. She'd think about how they were both risking their lives to save a child for a man they hardly knew. She'd think of Kam…

Kam…

She snuggled closer…

'Jen, I want you to wake up but quietly.'

Kam held her, speaking into her ear, his hand ready to close over her mouth if she made a startled noise. He already had the child awake, sitting close beside the pile of mats, his big eyes even wider now Kam had explained what they were doing.

'Jen, can you hear me? I know you're tired, but I need you to wake up.'

She stirred and turned her head, and even in the dim light of the cave the golden hair made a glorious tangle all around it. She'd have to hide it in her scarf because the moonlight would give it a glow that could be seen for miles.

'Come on, we're leaving,' he whispered, helping her to sit up. 'Tie your hair up as best you can and put your scarf around it. I'll carry your sandals, we'll go barefoot at first. And we'll leave your bag. I've written in the note that we'll come back tomorrow, but if we leave the bag they'll know we mean it. I've also given them my radio call-sign so they can contact us if there is a problem sooner than evening.'

She seemed to understand for her hands were fighting with her hair, trying to get hanks of it, uncombed, to braid. Then she lifted her shawl and wound it around her head and across the lower part of her face, a clever woman working out that her pale skin might also gleam in the moonlight.

A clever woman, but was he leading her to her death?

Kam didn't know, but he knew he had to try to get her out of here. If he left her and by some ill-chance the young mother died then they would kill Jen as well, or hold *her* for ransom, trading her for guns to keep the killing going. That she, who only sought to do good, and who had already suffered so much, should be put in such a position…

They had to leave.

He walked to the door of the cave, checked the man who had been left to guard them was sleeping then, taking Hamid on his back, he motioned Jen to fall in behind him and led the way, guided only by his childhood memories, praying they were right and that he wasn't leading two innocent people into disaster.

They slipped like shadows through the sleeping village, tension coiling tighter with every slip on a stone or brush against a branch, noises almost silent but sounding loud in the still night air. He waited for an alarm, a cry from a sentry posted somewhere in the village, although he judged the chief was confident in this, his stronghold.

'Do you really know the way?' Jenny asked when they were far enough above the village for her whisper not to carry.

'Of course I do.' Such a confident lie, but what was the sense in both of them worrying? 'We're on a path—can't you see that?'

'On a path made by sheep and goats and herders going up to the higher slopes, I would say from the look of it.'

He turned back to look at her and saw that she was smiling. His heart tugged at its moorings in his chest. How could she smile, this woman in a foreign land, being led through the mountains by someone who might not know the way, a child they had to cherish between the two of them?

And how could he not admire her, even, given the tug, feel more than admiration?

Feel love?

'It branches off,' he said, because to tell her what he was thinking and feeling would make the thoughts and feelings real, and neither of them wanted that.

When love between them was impossible…

They walked swiftly but quietly, climbing ever higher, the little boy walking now, stoically silent although the climb through the thinning air must be taking a toll on his slight body.

'Ten miles you said?' Jen asked the question when they stopped to rest beside a spring and Kam cupped water in his hand and made them both drink. 'I don't know how long it takes to walk ten miles on flat ground, let alone climbing through mountains in the moonlight.'

Kam smiled at her.

'I doubt it takes longer in the moonlight. In fact, it might make the journey faster for we can see where we are going and the night is cool. Come on, if we rest too long you'll stiffen up.'

'Or someone following us might catch up,' Jen suggested.

'There's no one following, not yet,' Kam said, knowing he'd have heard any pursuit because he'd been listening intently for it.

They climbed higher and higher until it seemed they were right at the top of the world—seemed they could touch the stars that massed like sparkling crystals in the velvet dark sky above them—yet still another ridge would rise in front of them.

The track wound and twisted, in and out of moonlight and shadows, sometimes wide enough for them to walk abreast, sometimes in single file. It was so quiet and still it was easy to think they were the only people alive in the entire world.

Until suddenly, as they entered a patch of shadow, a figure rose up from the ground, tall, dark-robed, head swathed in a turban—threatening just to look at.

Jen gave a cry, quickly stifling it with her hand, but she knew it hadn't been quick enough. She pressed her hand to her chest where her heart thudded so hard she thought it might burst out, then Kam was speaking and the shadowy figure answered, before stepping forward and squatting down to take Hamid on his back.

'You can't let him take Hamid,' Jen protested, racing towards the man to snatch the child from him. 'Not now when we've got this far.'

Kam stopped her, his hand settling on her shoulder and bringing her momentum to a halt.

'It's our guide,' Kam said. 'He says he knew we'd try to leave and has come to help us, to show us the way and carry the child. He doesn't like it that his chief would not honour the word he gave so he will honour it himself.'

'And you believe him? If Akbar was whipped for crossing the border, imagine what the chief would do to this man for betrayal. Why should he lead us where he says? Why wouldn't he make us circle around so we'll be right back in the village once again?'

'He gave his word. I trust him,' Kam said, then added with a tinge of sarcasm, 'Although there's not a lot of trust around.'

Was he referring to her suspicions of him—her questions as to whether he was a spy?

Jen didn't know, any more than she knew the truth about Kam's presence in the camp or their guide's offer to lead them home. She sighed at all the things she didn't know and followed, trudging along in the footsteps of the guide, Kam right behind her, barely puffing, the ease with which he climbed making her even angrier.

The path levelled out and they walked between high rock

walls and along a narrow track with a steep drop to one side of it, then, barely noticeable at first, they began to drop lower, going downhill now, down and down until they rounded a corner and there, still a hundred or more feet below them, lay the refugee camp.

Their guide set Hamid back on his feet, spoke to Kam, then disappeared back in the direction from which they'd come.

'He must return to his home before dawn or the chief will be suspicious,' Kam explained to Jen, as he took over as leader on the downhill path. 'He'll meet us where the vehicle was parked at six this evening, so that way we can get back before it gets too late.'

If we get back, Jen thought, but she didn't want to go there, so she questioned instead how the man could return to the village so swiftly.

'Before dawn?' she echoed, nodding towards the east where the sky was already lightening.

'He will run, now we're not with him,' Kam explained, then he knelt and took Hamid on his back and they continued towards their temporary home.

'Four hours,' Kam announced when they finally reached the clinic tent and stopped outside while Hamid crept in to be reunited with his parents, the wailing and cries of delight telling them all was well. 'Not bad for a ten-mile hike over the mountains.'

'Tell my feet that,' Jen said, lifting one sandalled foot to inspect it for wear and tear.

'Come, there'll be hot water in the food tent—we'll get something to eat and drink.'

'A hot drink? Food? That sounds like bliss. Come on, feet, it's only a little further.'

She turned towards the tent but Kam was quicker, lifting her into his arms and striding with her towards the tent, already lit to welcome the early risers in the camp.

Despite her weight, he held her easily, carrying her as though she were a child like Hamid. And with his strong arms holding her and her body pressed against his rock-hard chest, a sense of security, so strong she tingled with it, washed through her body.

At least, she hoped it was security…

Once in the tent he sat her on a mat and spoke to the women who were preparing food and drinks. One came immediately, a basin in her hands, a towel over her arm, and knelt in front of Jenny.

Kam thanked her and sent her on her way, removing Jenny's sandals himself then lifting one pale, slim foot, washing it, drying it, massaging it gently, then examining it for cuts or blisters before setting it back on the ground, to take care of the other.

'You'll put some antiseptic on the cuts and blisters when you go back to your tent,' he told her, still looking at her feet so it wasn't until she made a little sound of pain or protest that he looked up into her face.

She was staring at him as if she'd never seen him before, the look on her face so incredulous he wondered if he'd changed from a human into a djinn.

'What?' he asked, puzzled by her expression, but all she'd do was shake her head. Although he thought a smile was on its way, quivering at the corners of her lips, it did no more than tantalise him by not fully revealing itself.

He turned his attention from lips to feet.

'Do you have some soft slippers you can wear today?'

He looked up at her again, but all suggestion of a smile had disappeared and she was now frowning at him.

Before he could question her again—this time about the frown—the woman returned, bringing a tray with hot sweet tea and small pancakes, freshly made, their spicy scent making his mouth water.

'I didn't realise how hungry I was,' Jenny said, taking one of them, folding it in quarters, then eating it with obvious enjoyment. She took a sip of tea, and sighed.

'This is good,' she said, then looked at Kam. 'All good— the foot care, the food, the tea, not to mention your rescue efforts bringing us home over the mountains. Did I thank you?'

None of which explained the frown.

'I don't want your thanks,' he said, wondering how to ask about the frown, but no words came so he ate a pancake and drank some tea, then, because she hadn't answered about soft slippers, he asked one of the serving women if there was anyone in the camp who could sew the slippers the women wore inside their homes during the winter. He had a thick shirt they could use for fabric…

He washed my feet!

Jen wasn't sure whether to laugh or cry because the gesture, as much as his gentle touch, had totally destroyed any barriers she had tried to build between this man and her heart. With that one simple act of kindness she had awoken once again to love.

This man could well have saved her life tonight, leading her over the mountains, and she hadn't fallen in love with him then.

But as he'd washed her feet…

He couldn't know, of course, and neither could she reveal it. But how to hide a feeling that was bubbling like a spring of delight, and excitement, and happiness inside her?

With practicality, of course…

And distance…

And pretence…

'Well, we have Hamid back with his parents, and for that reason alone the walk was worth it,' she said, taking another pancake from the stack, folding it carefully and this time dipping it in flavoured yoghurt before biting into it. 'But might we have angered the chief to the extent that he will be more careful in his guarding of us tonight?'

'You do not have to go back,' Kam told her, his voice stern. 'I can go. I can treat the woman.'

Jen shook her head.

'I gave my word. We expect them to keep their side of the bargain, so how could I not go? Besides, that young woman, she's barely more than a girl, Kam, she might be upset or frightened, and a strange man around would make that worse. In fact, you don't need to come at all now we know the chief has such good English. He can translate.'

'Translate things about post-partum bleeding to another woman in his tribe? I don't think so. And that *is* the type of thing you might have to discuss.'

Jen shook her head.

'The women there are capable and experienced. One of them at least is a competent midwife, I'm sure of that. She will have explained things to the young mother and she'll watch to see the baby feeds. It's just the risk of infection in the wound or internally that bothers me. I need to go to check for that, but you needn't come. In fact, I'm probably safer on my own, because if two go they can keep one of us as ransom for the other to return, as they intended doing with Hamid.'

Kam heard the words, even heard sense in some of them,

but if Jenny thought he'd let her go over that border alone, she was mistaken.

That was thought number one.

Thought number two was more a question—what lay behind this sudden rush of common-sense words from a thoroughly exhausted woman? Why was she discussing this at all when she should be finishing her breakfast then having a sleep before beginning, belatedly, her day's work?

He sensed something beneath the words, some hidden reason for them, but maybe that was because so much about him was also hidden. She'd talked of her suspicions of him, and he'd parried them, but now he wished with all his heart that he hadn't had to lie to her—or maybe not lie, but at the least conceal the truth. Especially now they'd talked so much of trust.

'OK, that's breakfast done,' she said, looking up at him and smiling, but it was an open friendly smile, not the hidden one he'd hoped to see earlier, peeping out almost shyly. 'I'm going to follow my cup of tea with a couple of belts of coffee and that way I'll get through to afternoon. I'll feel better tonight if I have a nap this afternoon.'

Kam didn't protest, although when she'd finished a small cup of coffee and bent over to put her sandals back on he stopped her.

'Wait.'

He looked towards the serving woman who told him her friend had gone to get the slippers.

'Wait for what? What's going on?' Jen asked, and Kam smiled at her, reminding her of the need for distance and pretence.

'You didn't answer me about soft slippers,' he said. 'Someone is making some for you.'

'Someone is making me slippers? Making slippers while I ate breakfast? That's impossible!'

But the other woman had returned and she now came towards Jen, shyly offering a pair of the prettiest slippers Jen had ever seen. A deep maroon, a colour she knew came from the dye of a local desert plant, and decorated with embroidered flowers.

Kam took them from the woman, exchanging words, then he slipped them on Jen's feet.

'They feel as smooth as velvet,' she whispered, wriggling her toes to luxuriate in the softness.

'They're made from felted camel hair,' Kam explained. 'I think young girls learn to make slippers almost as soon as they learn to walk, and there always seems to be someone making them in every camp.'

'They're beautiful,' Jen said, pointing her toes in front of her the better to admire them. 'Will you thank her for me, and thank whoever gave them to her? Should I offer to pay—to buy them?'

Kam smiled again, the smile slipping over the broken barriers around her heart and touching it with happiness.

'You'd insult them if you offered to pay and, of course, I thanked them. And now, Dr Stapleton, let's get you home— you can't walk across the sand with those pretty feet.'

He bent and lifted her again and although she wanted to protest—should protest, she could have worn her sandals across the sand between the tents—she didn't, content to steal a few minutes in his arms, impersonal though they may be.

He had to stop carrying her, Kam realised as he held her against his chest and felt his heart beating with desire. Oh, that he could be carrying her into his own tent, a beautiful woman he'd claimed as his!

Of course, he didn't have a tent, and this particular beautiful woman certainly wasn't his.

She couldn't be his, she of the wanderlust and he in need of a stay-at-home wife...

He set her down inside the big tent, and was pleased to see Lia and Akbar sitting with Hamid between them, the little boy prattling on about his adventures, the parents happy just to have him there.

When Akbar saw Kam he did nothing more than nod, but the nod said a thousand things that words could never have said. Kam nodded back, understanding between the two of them, though Lia had to put her thanks and happiness into words, a stream of them, until Akbar held up his hand for silence then announced he was moving back to his own tent now.

'He's leaving?' Jenny asked, as Lia helped her husband stand and a conversation she couldn't follow went on between the men.

'They want to be in their own tent,' Kam explained, and Jenny nodded.

'I can understand that. They want to be a family. You will tell him to call in each day so we can check his wounds.'

Kam smiled at the anxiety in her voice.

'I will,' he promised, not telling her he'd already given Akbar this advice, only he'd suggested every second day. Jenny was more anxious than he was, worrying that any adverse consequences in the camp might jeopardise her TB programme.

Jenny headed for her corner of the tent, knowing her hair must be like a bird's nest beneath the shawl still wrapped loosely around it, knowing her body needed a break from Kam's proximity while her heart needed to recover from his gift of slippers, for she knew he must have asked for them and probably would pay for them.

Wasn't there a bumper sticker back in the real world about senseless acts of kindness? That's all these were, she told herself. Washing her feet, finding slippers for them—it meant nothing more than kindness. It was her folly that they turned her heart to mush…

She dragged the brush through her tangled hair, letting it pull at the knots, thinking pain might help restore some common sense. It didn't work, her heart beating faster as she heard Kam talking to Marij or Aisha as they began the morning testing.

At least she'd got the knots out with her efforts, so now she could plait it, then a quick wash, a change of clothes and she'd be ready to start the day.

A deep sigh started way down near the pretty slippers and escaped in a rush of air. Had it only been twelve hours ago she'd stood here, washing, and wishing she could change into something pretty, worrying that her meeting with Kam on the rock would look too much like a date if she did?

Some date!

She washed, dressed then joined the two nurses, noticing as she passed that Kam had set up a kind of clinic near the doorway of the tent and was tending what looked like a deep cut on one of the small boys who hung around her most of the time.

Detouring towards them, she realised the rest of the boys were hanging back.

'What happened?' she asked Kam, as she drew closer and saw the jagged cut that slashed across the child's forearm.

Kam turned to her and smiled then motioned the other boys closer.

'Did you ever swear allegiance to a gang? Become a blood brother, or in your case a blood sister? Your boys have formed a—I suppose club is a better word than gang, and had to mingle blood to take their oath. Problem was, the only knife they had was a kitchen one and it was blunt, so they used the top of a tin can and Ahmed here went a little deep.'

Jen wasn't sure if smiling was the right response, but she was fond of the boys and they were now eyeing her warily, so she did smile, then said to Kam, 'It's not dangerous, this club, is it? I wouldn't like them to be swearing blood oaths to maim or kill or steal or do anything bad. Without school to attend, they could get up to all kinds of mischief.'

Kam finished winding a bandage around the now cleaned wound and sent the boys off with a warning to be careful, and it was only as they turned to go that she realised one of them was carrying Rosana on his back.

'You want to know what their blood oath was?' Kam asked, smiling so broadly Jen knew it wasn't bad, although the way the smile made her feel fitted the description only too well.

She nodded, and his smile became a chuckle.

'They've adopted Rosana,' he said. 'The oath was to protect her at all times, both now and all through her life. That little girl has got herself a family, even if they are all nine or ten. They'll grow up and so will she, and pity help any young man who might fancy her later on. He'll have to run the gauntlet of those boys, and really prove himself worthy— What's wrong?'

Jen shook her head, aware tears were seeping from her eyes and slipping down her cheeks but unable to stop them.

'They are so good—there is so much goodness,' she finally managed, swiping at the tears that still escaped her brimming eyes. 'Here in a place where people have so little, and where hope is close to dying, those little boys have pledged to help that child…'

Kam could not help himself. He pulled Jenny into his arms, steered her into the relative privacy of the space she called her bedroom and held her close, rocking her in his arms until he felt the tension ease out of her.

He tilted her chin and looked down at her face, using his handkerchief to wipe the dampness from her cheeks.

'How can you do this work when you feel the pain of others so strongly?' he asked, his voice gentle but bemused.

'How can I not do this work?' she replied, offering him a strained smile. 'When I see the problems other people have, how can I not do something, however small, to help?'

She kissed him lightly on the lips, readjusted her scarf and slipped away from him.

CHAPTER EIGHT

JENNY worked hard through the morning, uninterrupted by the usual requests for medical help as Kam was seeing those who felt sick or were injured in some way. She wanted the slides done and the medications put out by early afternoon, so she could have a sleep before returning to the rebel camp.

The thought brought a slightly grim smile to her lips. One night of adventure and she was considering this return to the other side of the border as calmly as she'd catch a train to the city back home in Brisbane.

Better than considering other consequences, she decided, although a slight tremor of apprehension in her abdomen suggested she didn't feel quite as blasé as she'd like to be. The chief *could* keep them there. Or he might be so angered by them leaving the previous night, he would kill them.

Somehow, Jenny thought not. Regardless of the cause of the fighting, the chief was intelligent enough to know they weren't part of it, and that making them part of it could bring retribution down not only on his head but on the heads of his people.

'No more patients, so I'll help with the slides.'

Kam settled himself beside her, causing consternation in her lungs and happy little leaps of delight in her heart.

She concentrated on the consternation.

'You didn't come to help me out but to check the needs of the place and start a medical clinic. Have you contacted your brother? Asked him about a tent for it? Mentioned a well?'

Kam took a group of red-marked slides and slid the first onto the plate of the microscope.

'I've spoken to my brother,' he said, knowing it wasn't the reply Jenny wanted but unwilling to tell her a lie and unable to tell her he'd done no more than say he was alive and his research was going more slowly than he'd expected.

Not exactly a lie but there was no way he could leave until Jenny's trips across the border had ceased.

Unless, of course, he could provide her with a suitable escort, but who?

And as far as the well and other things were concerned, he was aware that radio messages could be monitored easily and hadn't wanted to alert the rebels over the border to the fact that he might be a person of power. If he'd spoken of the camp's needs, Arun would immediately have got things moving, and the chief in the captured village might begin to wonder. And mention of their adventure of the previous evening would undoubtedly bring Arun rushing to the mountains, a complication Kam didn't want to think about.

Not least because his brother had a way with women, an ease about him that drew women in, so a mild flirtation led to something more very quickly…

Suffice it to say he didn't want his playboy brother anywhere in Jenny's vicinity. Not for selfish reasons, he told himself, but because he'd sensed a vulnerability in her from their first meeting, and now to know she'd lost her husband and unborn child…

'Have you gone to sleep there, or is there something on the slide I should know about?'

Jenny's question jerked him back to the present.

'No, this one's good. I put it where?'

She showed him and continued writing notes for medication, but working so close to her was distracting, while thinking of her crossing the border again tonight—

Gut-knotting—there was no other word for it.

'I think I'll check the boys,' he said, and stood up, knowing he couldn't stay beside her without trying to persuade her not to go. Yet he knew, short of tying her to a tent peg, there was no way to stop her.

Stubborn woman!

Beautiful woman…

'Thanks for all your help,' she said, as he eased away.

'Sarcastic woman!' he said aloud, then hurried from the tent.

Jen was glad he'd gone. Having him so close had been distracting, to say the least.

He'd washed her feet!

She *had* to stop that thought recurring in her mind. Surely if she wanted to think of his kindness she should be thinking of the way he'd sheltered her as she'd slept the previous night, his arm around her shoulders, the air between them zinging with the attraction they'd both now admitted, but him understanding her halting explanation of inexperience and honouring her wish to not take the attraction further.

'You go,' Marij said to her an hour later, when the daily medications had been given out and the testing finished. 'Aisha and I will do the rest. We can put the slides together and we know the medication plan as well as you do. You go and sleep.'

Aisha looked as worried as she sounded.

'I'm not that tired,' Jen told her. 'I think doctors get enough early training of sleepless nights to be able to handle them with ease.'

'I do not worry over your lack of sleep,' the nurse replied. 'I worry about you going back to that place again tonight. It is dangerous. It is stupid that you go. And that man who goes with you has not the sense of a rabbit that he lets you go. Look at what they did to Akbar.'

'They thought he was going to steal from them—he did not tell them about Hamid in case they hurt the boy. I suppose he was lucky he was only flogged, not dealt some far worse punishment.'

Aisha shuddered.

'You are right, although I think even over there they are no longer barbarians who would cut off the hand of a thief.'

Jen joined in the shuddering, but was quick to reassure Aisha that she'd be all right.

'They want me healthy and with both my hands,' Jen joked, 'so I can look after the new mother. Just pray there are no complications.'

'I will pray for you,' Aisha said, and Jen knew she would. 'Now, go and sleep.'

Jen obeyed the order this time, suddenly so tired it was the only thing to do. Who knew what mistakes she might have made if she'd stayed there?

She woke at five, her internal alarm in perfect working order, and found her water containers full and her wash basin already filled with water for her wash.

The little boys or Kam?

Deciding it didn't matter but thankful that she didn't have to fetch it herself, she stripped off, found a towel to stand on, then soaped herself all over. After three years with Aid for All, she was an expert at bird-baths, as she called her splash, soap and rinse routine, and now rinsed off all the soap and dried herself, pleased to know the rose scent of the soap lingered on her skin.

Now, what to wear? The long tunics she put over her jeans were fairly tight fitting, and the one she'd been wearing had hampered her as she'd climbed the mountain the previous night, but jeans on their own weren't the answer for a visit to the rebel camp. She opened her suitcase and dug to the bottom, pulling out a long full skirt she'd bought at a market in Colombia. It was black but a wide band around the bottom of it was decorated with beads and braid, making it a little festive. A long-sleeved blouse, also black, would complete her outfit and with a scarf around her hair, she'd almost pass as a local. Well, not quite almost...

She dressed then brushed her hair, a refrain—should get it cut—accompanying each stroke. Not that she would, for her hair having grown it since the accident, was the symbol of her new life...

Kam was waiting outside, and for a moment she thought she saw admiration in his eyes, but he made no comment on her clothing, simply nodding to her then leading her swiftly through the camp towards the place where they were to meet their guide.

'I've some bread and water in my backpack,' he told her, 'but I think with us coming at this hour, they will offer us food.'

An idle conversation but there was something bothering him, so when he paused and looked around the camp and then up at the sky, she asked, 'What's wrong? Something other than us going back across the border? What else is worrying you?'

'There's a storm coming,' he said, then continued on his way, leaving Jen to follow.

Which she did, although she, too, looked up at the sky as she walked. No sign of clouds but, then, there was no sign of the sky either. A hazy greyness, so pale it was almost white, was all she could see.

'There are no clouds,' she pointed out, as she caught up with him again.

'But what do you see?' he asked.

'Haze? We get heat haze in the summer—is this the same?'

He shook his head.

'This haze is caused by dust—there's a sandstorm brewing.'

'I've heard of them, but does that matter? We'll be in a vehicle, we'll still be able to get there and back, won't we?'

This time he smiled as he shook his head.

'Windscreen wipers don't clear dust from the windscreen, and sand in a storm can strip a car of paint—that's how fierce these storms can be.'

Jen looked around again but the haze didn't seem any worse than it had minutes earlier. She was thinking of asking what was the worst that could happen if the storm did come when they rounded the last corner of the camp and saw the vehicle ahead of them.

'Oh, Kam, it's our same guide,' she said, grabbing her companion's arm to share her delight. 'I've been so worried he might be in trouble and been beaten or had his hands cut off or something.'

'Hands cut off?' Kam echoed, stopping to turn back and look at her.

'Something Aisha said,' Jen explained, aware her smile was growing broader by the second. 'Please, tell him how glad we are to see him and ask if he and his family are all well, so we know there've been no repercussions.'

Kam spoke to the man who bowed and smiled at Jenny then the conversation must have shifted to the possibly approaching storm for both men were looking upwards and pointing to the sky.

She climbed into the back seat of the vehicle while the men spoke, and settled the small bag she'd brought with her on her lap. Women all around the camp had heard about the baby's birth and had brought small presents for it, including a tiny pair of embroidered slippers.

She'd asked Marij why people would send gifts to the baby of tribesmen who had forced the refugees from their home, and Marij had smiled.

'The baby is a new life, innocent,' she said. 'The baby is not to blame for what has happened.'

And even thinking about the conversation made Jen's eyes water and her nose go snuffly. What was wrong with her that she was becoming sentimental over such small incidents?

Was it the baby?

She pressed her hand against her own belly, remembering it swollen and hard as a melon, eight months pregnant when the accident had taken not only David but their unborn son.

Maudlin—that's how she was getting, and she had to get over it.

Fast!

Kam and the driver had climbed into the front seats and to distract her mind from maudlin she tapped Kam on the shoulder.

'Was he in trouble with the chief?' she asked.

Kam shook his head.

'The chief thinks we made our way over the mountains on our own, possibly with Hamid guiding us.'

The chief didn't exactly think that, Kam knew, but didn't say so. The chief, according to their guide, was very suspicious and because he would know a foreign woman wouldn't find her way across the mountains, his suspicions undoubtedly rested on Kam.

However, suspicions, imagined or otherwise, were the least of everyone's problems right now. Their guide agreed that a sandstorm was on the way, and even as they drove Kam could feel the wind picking up, blowing sand against the car, dust settling on the windscreen.

By the time they reached the women's tent in the village, the wind was whistling and the sand keening as it swept across the desert's surface. Soon it would scream, Kam knew. Soon anyone outside would be lost and disoriented, unable to move until the storm subsided.

Which could take days…

They stopped outside the women's tent and Jenny got out. She hurried in, the sand and wind blustering about her, plucking at her skirt as though unseen hands were grabbing it.

'You have come.'

The chief was with his wife, Jenny's medical bag beside him, the women of the tent far back against the walls, which were all wound down and no doubt pegged because, although they ballooned in and out, they held fast.

'I said I'd come and I will come again. I have kept my word so I expect you to keep yours, and let me go when I have done my job. There may be no need for me to see her every day, but until her wound is healed I will keep coming.'

The chief nodded but, understanding more now about oaths and agreements, Jen knew this meant little. Until he shook hands there'd be no agreement he had to honour, and he probably wouldn't shake hands with a woman anyway. Jen would have to leave those negotiations to Kam.

But she did have something in the way of peace offerings. She knelt beside the woman who held her sleeping baby in her arms and began to undo the string on the small bag she'd carried.

'No!' the chief ordered, snatching the bag from her hands.

'Hey, it's OK. You should know I wouldn't harm your wife or your baby—or anyone's wife or baby, for that matter. The women from the camp have sent gifts for the baby. I was going to show them to your wife.'

The chief, who'd by now had time to examine the contents of Jenny's bag, had the grace to look embarrassed.

'They are kind and the gifts are thoughtful,' he admitted, then spoke to his wife, spreading out the gifts in front of her.

She touched each in turn, smiling and looking from them to the baby, then packed them back into the bag and set it beside her.

'How is your wife feeling?' Jen asked, trying to pretend everything was all right, although the chief's sudden, angry reaction earlier had frightened her.

'She is in pain but the tablets help, also the ice. This will take some time?'

'Like all wounds,' Jenny explained, 'it will take time to heal, both inside and outside.'

The man nodded then repeated Jenny's words to his wife.

'May I examine her?' Jen said. 'I need to check the wound to see there's no infection and to take her blood pressure, temperature and pulse to make sure everything is mending as it should.'

The man translated for his wife, then called a woman forward. It was the woman Jen had assumed was the midwife.

'I need to talk to her about women's medical matters,' Jen told the chief. 'Perhaps you would prefer it if my colleague translated these.'

The man looked from Jenny to his wife, then back to Jenny.

'He will remain outside the tent and I will wait with him. I could do the translation, you understand, but it would not be right for me to speak to a woman of my tribe of such matters.'

He spoke again to his wife, kissed her forehead then left the tent, leaving his little bride looking insecure and nervous again.

'Are you there, Kam?' Jen asked, and when he answered, she began, explaining first that she was going to examine the woman, beginning with the regular observations.

'Will you tell her this is normal and there's no need to be afraid? She's nervous and unsettled without her husband here, and I don't want to upset her more.'

Kam spoke, then the chief chimed in, and Jen hoped he was repeating the reassurances.

Smiling encouragingly at her patient, Jenny began the tests, pleased to see no elevated temperature, no raised pulse or irregularities in her blood pressure.

'All good,' she reported to Kam, then, with the help of the other woman, she unwrapped her patient and examined first her breasts for signs of soreness or milk fever.

'Will you ask the midwife if the baby is feeding from the breast and if the woman's milk has come in yet? It may be a bit early, but it's best to know so we can watch for any trouble.'

Kam and Jenny's helper conversed for quite a time, then Kam reported all was well and that they could be confident the midwife knew her job, having helped more than two hundred babies into the world and watched over the mothers and their infants for forty days and nights after the birth.

'It is a time the women spend with other women,' Kam explained. 'The chief being with his wife is an exception and he is only there to reassure her, leaving her to the women most of the time.'

'That's good,' Jen said, smiling at the new mother, who now looked slightly more confident.

Carefully, Jen undid the dressings on the wound, asking for more light so she could examine it more closely, seeking any signs of redness or weeping from infection. It looked clean and she asked Kam to check the woman was taking her antibiotics as well as painkillers.

'Of course she is,' the chief replied. 'I see to it she does. I do not want her sick.'

'The wound looks good,' Jen reported, and saw the midwife's smile as Kam repeated it. Then the woman spoke, words tripping off her tongue, while Jen applied new antiseptic to the wound and dressed it with clean dressings.

'She's asking if she can learn to do the operation. She said it looked easy and many women in the tribe have died because a doctor couldn't come and do it when a baby becomes stuck.'

Jen squatted back on her heels, straining to hear Kam's voice as the wind was now whipping against the tent walls and echoing around the camp with an eerie, wailing sound.

'I know a number of midwives back at home whom I would be happy to have do it, but there's the anaesthetic as well. Are there many tribal people in these parts on both sides of the border? Would it be possible to set up a course for the midwives to learn enough to do a Caesarean?'

'Boy, are you getting into delicate ground!' Kam said.

'You, a doctor, suggesting a nurse might be able to do doctor stuff as well as any doctor.'

'Or better,' Jenny told him. 'There's no reason why not. After all, we train paramedics to do emergency trauma work, so why not train midwives to do Caesars?'

'Why not indeed?' Kam said, and Jenny smiled as she heard him translating their conversation to the midwife. At least, that's what she thought he was doing.

Finished with her examination of the mother, she asked if she could look at the baby. Once the request was translated, the young mother displayed him proudly, unwrapping his swaddling garments so Jen could see him.

'He's beautiful,' she said, awed as ever by the miniature perfection of new life, saddened as ever by her own loss.

The girl-woman glowed with pride and happiness and held the infant to her breast where he nuzzled for a moment then began to feed.

Jen wanted to ask about the customs here, about feeding times and habits, but she knew the chief might find the conversation awkward if it was carried on in front of him so she assured him that all was well and packed her bag, ready to leave.

Kam met her outside the doorway of the tent, a worried frown warning her there was something very wrong.

'What is it?' she asked.

'Can't you see?'

She was still within the porch-like area at the entrance to the tent, outside the inner wall but still sheltered, but now she did look outside at the thick dust cloud swirling beyond the outer wall.

'The storm?'

'The storm!' Kam confirmed. 'We can't go back tonight.'

He didn't add that storms like this could last for days, because he didn't want Jen worrying. 'The chief has suggested we eat dinner with him then sleep again in the cave dwelling. He has had his men put some provisions in there and rugs across the entrance. They will keep out some of the dust, but in a storm like this it gets everywhere. You breathe it and eat it and sleep with it in your bed, no matter how hard you try to keep it out.'

He watched Jenny's face as she took this in, then drew her closer to adjust her scarf around her head so it also covered her face.

'Come,' he said, taking her hand in his. 'We're going to run. Stay close behind me.'

They ran, Kam regretting he hadn't taken the scarf the chief had offered him. Wound around his face, it would have prevented the stinging sand from burning his skin, but he feared that if he wore it he might be more recognisable than he was in a baseball cap.

A foolish fear, perhaps, but one he wasn't going to put to the test.

Once at the chief's meeting tent, he slipped off his shoes and helped Jenny off with her sandals, before leading her inside. Their guide was there and other men, already seated on rugs on the ground, helping themselves to food from a huge pot in the middle of the rug.

'You will eat,' the chief told them, and Kam served a dish of stew for Jenny, gave it to her with some bread, then helped himself as well. He was uneasy, the storm an unexpected complication. How long might they have to remain in this place?

Would Arun, hearing of the storm, accept that radio transmissions would be difficult and not come riding to his rescue?

Kam ate, but barely tasted his meal, and when he saw that

Jenny had finished hers, he excused himself to the chief and took Jen's arm to help her to her feet.

'You didn't want to stay and chat?' she teased, when they were putting their sandals back on in the entry-way and gathering strength to once again venture out into the swirling, dancing, deadly sand.

'I wanted to get you safely in the cave,' he told her, then his body leapt as the implications of the statement brought excitement to it.

Too bad! His body was used enough to celibacy to get over its excitement, though being stuck in a cave with Jenny Stapleton while a sandstorm whirled outside, possibly for days, would sorely tempt it.

Once again he adjusted Jenny's scarf, wishing he'd asked one of the women to find a shawl for her so he could better protect the tender skin on her face from the onslaught of the sand.

But something was better than nothing and when he was convinced he'd covered as much of her face as he safely could, he took her hand, told her to stay behind him and ventured out.

Jenny realised as soon as they stepped out of the lee of the tent that the storm had become much worse. She put a hand to her face to shield her eyes and followed close behind Kam.

The air was filled with red, gritty dust, whirling and eddying angrily all around them. She saw vague shapes she guessed were tents or houses and prayed Kam knew where they were going.

The ducked along alleyways, staying close to walls in the lee of the wind, but already sand drifts were building up against fences and walls in the way she imagined snow would build up against the walls of houses during a snowstorm.

'We're here,' Kam said, and held a rug a little to one side so she could duck inside the cave.

It was dark, but someone had left a lit lamp on a table at the back, beyond the mats where they'd slept for a short time the previous night.

Jen walked towards the light, feeling sand inside all her clothes, wishing she could take them off and shake them but shy in front of Kam.

'Oh!' she said, when she approached the table. There, set out for them, or maybe just for her, was a hairbrush, soap and a jar of what looked like face cream and smelt of roses, a clean robe she could wear to bed, and a selection of shawls and scarves.

At the other end of the table was a small spirit stove, a kettle, cups, flat bread wrapped in cloth and some canned goods, but most surprising of all were the teabags, a whole packet of them.

'There's water in those drums in the corner, a basin to wash in, a privy behind the curtain, and we're all set up to play house,' Kam said, coming to stand behind her and examine the supplies for himself.

'Play house,' Jen echoed, and turned towards him, unwinding her scarf from her face as she did so. 'Did you play house as a child?'

He half smiled and rubbed his hand across his chin, and she saw where wind and sand had burnt his skin.

'I don't remember being a child.'

It was such a bleak statement Jen gasped then turned to take him in her arms, to hold him to her body as if that might in some way make amends.

They were too close!

Kam's lips found hers, sand and grit forgotten as they gave

in to the attraction that had simmered between them since they'd first met.

Jen remembered her brave words of the night before, about not being able to handle an affair, but they'd been spoken before Kam had washed her feet.

Now she knew that kisses between them were never going to be enough!

Not only knew but was longing for whatever followed, with a desire so strong it was like a pain, both in her chest, and abdomen, and right down to the apex of her thighs, a pain that throbbed in time to the beating of her heart, a pain that could only be alleviated in one way...

CHAPTER NINE

KAM broke the embrace.

'We'll not rush into this,' he said, tilting her face so he could look into her eyes. 'You're sure?'

Jen nodded because a bald yes might have sounded too clinical somehow, and this, as far as she was concerned, was about love. Not that Kam would ever know it, but if her voice had trembled when she said yes he might wonder.

'So let's get the sand out of our clothes and off our bodies. Are you shy of me, Jenny? If so, I'll pour a basin of water for you and set it in the corner of the cave so you can wash in privacy, or I could help you undress and shake the sand from your clothes, and wash your back...'

He was giving her a choice. It was too much. Jen shook her head then nodded, and saw Kam smile.

'Let's start with the scarf, shall we?' he said gently, and he unwound the scarf he'd wrapped around her head. Then he slipped the band from the bottom of her plait and set it on the table, picking up the brush as he unwound her hair.

'If you only knew how often I've dreamt of doing this,' he whispered, beginning to brush her hair with long, firm strokes. 'It has tempted and tantalised me, that plait.'

Jen tingled from his ministrations but knew she had to get her emotions in some degree of order.

'It can't have been too often,' she reminded him. 'We've only known each other a couple of days.'

He smiled and kept on brushing.

'I daydream as well,' he said.

Eventually Kam was satisfied he'd rid her hair of most of the sand it had collected and he let her gather it and knot it on her head, then, his fingers shaking slightly, he undid the first button on her shirt, his eyes on her face to read her reaction, determined not to rush her if she showed the slightest hint of apprehension.

Her eyes met his and held them, so he continued to undo buttons, although he could feel her body trembling beneath the light cotton of her shirt, a trembling that increased as his fingers brushed against the swell of her breast. His own body was behaving badly, but he ignored it and kept going, eventually peeling the shirt off and taking it towards the door to give it a hard shake, then setting it on a ledge that ran along the side of the cave that had been dug out over centuries of summer visits from the tribes.

He turned back to find Jenny had taken off her skirt, without attempting to cover her body, although he guessed she must be longing to. She handed it to him to shake and set beside the shirt on the ledge.

Her bra and tiny bikini panties were both black, sensibly so considering the difficulties with laundry in a desert, yet they made her pale skin look even paler, and the sight of her, the swell of hips, the indentation of her slim waist, then her body swelling out again in full, heavy breasts, started a hunger so strong he had to hold himself back from taking her into his arms and tossing her on the pile of rugs that made up their bed.

'You are beautiful,' he managed, although the tightness in his throat strangled the words as they came out. 'Beautiful!'

She moved, taking the basin to the corner, filling it with water and, with her back to him, removing the rest of her clothes and soaping her scarf, using it to wash her body.

And even in the dim light Kam could see the fine tracings of the scars across her back, no doubt from the accident in which her husband had died.

So she'd suffered a double blow, and his heart ached for her, but heartache didn't stop the hunger…

He stripped off his jeans and shirt and picked up a towel and the jar of rose-scented cream. He came towards her slowly, as he would to a skittish horse unused to man's handling.

'Let me dry you,' he murmured, and although Jen started at his voice, when he touched her with the towel, she stood still. But rubbing cream into that pale skin, feeling her flesh beneath it and the curves and indentations of her body proved his undoing.

'If I keep this up, I'll shame myself,' he said, nodding towards his very obvious erection. 'You finish with the cream while I have a wash.'

Jen took the jar from his hands and moved across to the pile of rugs. The light was dim enough for her not to feel embarrassment, or was it because of the way she felt about Kam that such a negative emotion had no place in her mind?

She didn't know and neither did she waste thought on it for very long, contenting herself instead with rubbing the smooth, scented cream into the skin on her face and neck, enjoying the simple pleasure of pampering herself.

As for Kam…

She watched him as he washed, saw the strong shoulders

she knew he had because he'd carried her so easily, and the way his back tapered to a slim waist and hips, before swelling to a very attractive backside and strong, long legs.

Was it the unreality of the storm and the cave and the rebel camp that was making what lay ahead possible for her?

Or was it love?

She rather hoped it wasn't love pushing her into Kam's arms tonight. The love she felt for him should be separate to this. It would be far better for her peace of mind if she'd finally matured enough to take some pleasure from a chance meeting with a man to whom she felt attraction; if she'd matured enough to enjoy an affair and then forget it—or maybe not forget it but tuck the memory away somewhere safe—and move on with her life.

That way the love she felt for him could stay hidden in her heart, rather than leaking out and embarrassing both of them.

He turned towards her and she realised it was all academic anyway. She was about to make love—OK, have sex—with the most gorgeous man she'd ever seen, and her body was so excited it was a wonder he couldn't see her shaking from the other side of the cave.

But when he reached the pile of mats on which she sat, he lay down and propped himself on one elbow, frowning at her.

'What's wrong?' she said, reaching out her hand to take his and pull him down beside her.

He resisted her tug and continued frowning.

'I have no protection,' he muttered, as if both embarrassed and angered by this circumstance that had caught him in a cave in the desert in the middle of a sandstorm without a condom in his jeans pocket.

Jen squeezed his fingers, and tugged again.

'It's OK, I'm protected,' she told him, not adding what kind of protection—that of her inability to carry a child. The sadness of it hit her like it usually did, but not as strongly so she could let it pass. While it wasn't one hundred per cent certain, her doctors believed the internal injuries she'd suffered in the accident meant she would never conceive again.

'You are beautiful,' Kam repeated, finally sitting beside her and taking her into his arms, kissing her as he'd kissed her earlier, gently at first then with increasing passion until they were both shaking with the need to find the ultimate release.

Yet they held back, exploring with their hands, Jen rediscovering the delight of a hard male body, the contours of thick slabs of muscle, the smoothness of male skin. Kam's fingers traced her scars and he hissed beneath his breath, but the touch was so gentle it excited her more than it embarrassed her.

His hands roamed her body, touching it in secret places, setting it on fire, until she took the initiative and guided him inside her and they joined in a rhythm old as time itself and together found release, his gasp echoing her own cry of satisfaction as her body melted into a million quivering nerve cells before slowly reforming into human shape.

Sated, they lay together, silent by unspoken agreement, and finally Jen turned sleepily in Kam's arms and snuggled up against his body, letting sleep come, although the wailing of the wind outside and the splatter of sand against the mats was loud enough to wake the dead.

There was no night or day in the time that followed, just the crying of the wind, rising to shrieks and falling to moans, and the movement of the mats that formed their doorway, and desire, heating Jen's body and hammering in her heart. Was it the same for Kam?

She could only guess it was, for the simplest, slightest touch would have them back on the pile of mats that formed their bed, their bodies more familiar to each other now so pleasure came more easily, although held back at times so the ending would be all the sweeter.

'I can't believe this is happening,' she said, some time in what she thought might be their second night in the cave. 'All we do is make love and boil water for cups of tea.'

She was making a cup of tea as she spoke, naked as the day she'd been born and feeling no shame. It *had* to be because it was like a time out of life, a diversion from reality that would have no meaning in the future. What happened here in the cave would remain a secret held inside her, a memory to cherish and inspect from time to time, but never to regret.

'There's not much else to do in a sandstorm,' Kam told her, 'although I do need more sustenance than tea and bread. I think I'll open the cans and you can make us a nice stew from whatever's inside them.'

'Hey, I made the tea, you make the stew.'

He stared at her and Jen knew something had shifted between them.

'You can't make stew?' she said, hoping a light-hearted tease might shift things back again.

'I've never thought to do it,' he said, and somehow the distance grew even greater.

We've never talked about ourselves, Jen realised, the realisation bringing an icy shock. Apart from her mentioning David's death, they'd had no personal conversation. He could be married with five kids! What had she done? How could she have been so…uncaring?

Was this the way affairs worked?

She didn't know but wished she had her friend Melissa here—well, not right here but at the other end of a telephone—so she could ask.

But Melissa wasn't here and all the implications of not talking about personal things had struck her with a force that made her hands shake.

'We know nothing about each other,' she said, her voice strained as what ifs hammered in her head. 'What have I done? Is it because your wife cooks for you that you can't make a stew? Are you married, Kam? Have I been the cause of you being unfaithful to your wife? Or to someone who is important in your life? Why didn't I ask? How stupid could I be?'

He came towards her, his hands reaching out towards her, but she stepped back so he couldn't touch her, knowing his touch could make her forget her concerns—forget everything—and right now she needed answers, not oblivion.

She pulled on the gown that had been left for her to sleep in and, seeing the gesture, Kam wound the sarong he'd told her was called a *wezaar* around his waist.

The gestures—the covering of their bodies—said far more than words and emphasised the rift between them.

'I am not married and there's no one else in my life at the moment.' She could see his eyes, see the greenness, although the cave was dimly lit, and she read truth, but also something else in them.

Something else he wasn't long in revealing.

'Do you think so little of me you think I'd cheat on my wife? Or betray a special woman?'

Jen held out her hands.

'I don't know what to think, Kam,' she said helplessly.

'I've never been in this situation before, and things happened so quickly.'

This was the truth but not the whole truth. Inside Jen a tiny bud of hope had sprouted and was now swelling irrationally. He's not married, there's no one else, he washed my feet—could he not love me?

Couldn't love grow between us?

Stupid hope, she said mentally, determined to squelch it before it got too strong. Remember this is a time out of reality, a window into another world, open for a short space and soon to close again.

This isn't love.

Well, not on his side...

Kam had walked back to sit down on the mats, and all Jen wanted was for things to be right between them again.

But how to get from here to there?

With practicality, of course. And pretence. She would pretend she hadn't felt the shift, and that the marriage conversation hadn't happened. Go back to stew!

'Did you live at home when you were studying, that you never learnt to fend for yourself, shopping and cooking and such?'

'I studied first in London and then here. My family had a house in both cities and staff, of course, so, no, cooking for myself wasn't something I ever learnt.'

Staff, of course? Who had 'staff, of course' in this day and age?

Very, very, very wealthy people, that's who!

She stared at him as the little bud folded back on itself. Very rich people married other very rich people, not nobodies from Brisbane, Queensland, Australia.

Kam knew the time had come to tell Jenny the truth. How could he continue to lie—or if not to lie to deceive—a woman who had given herself so unselfishly and wholeheartedly to him, who had met his passion and matched it with her own, the little cries she'd uttered lingering at all times in his head? Memories of them were causing his body to stir even now when coolness lay between them.

'Come and sit beside me,' he said. 'I'll make do with tea and bread for now, then you can teach me to make stew.'

She came, handing him a cup of tea and a torn-off piece of now stale flat-bread.

'Maybe learn to make bread as well,' he joked, but she didn't smile, alerted by his tone that this was serious.

'Jen…' he began, then stalled.

How to tell her?

How to explain?

Should he begin with his father? With his illness and the gradual slide into decline his country had taken?

But he didn't want to blame his father, or blame anyone for his deceit, so…

'Jen,' he tried again, and this time found some of the words he needed. 'You were right to be suspicious of me.'

She got up so quickly her tea spilt.

'Sit!' he ordered. 'Let me explain.'

She sat again but she was trembling and he wanted to take her in his arms and hold her close until the trembling stopped, and then maybe for ever.

That last thought shocked him.

For ever meant love.

No way could he be in love with Jenny Stapleton—not now, with his country in turmoil, looking to the new ruler to make things right again. What would the people think of that new ruler marrying a foreigner? He'd lose all credibility. And on top of that, his mother was even now scouting for a suitable bride.

'So, are you going to explain?'

She'd stopped trembling and now sounded angry, angry enough for Kam to realise he'd been lost in his own thoughts for too long.

'I meant no harm, coming to the refugee camp as I did,' he began, 'and as for my name, it is somewhere near the truth because I've held a passport in the name of Kam Rahman since I was seven. That was how old I was when our father sent me and my twin brother Arun off to school in England. My full name is Kamid Rahman al'Kawali, so he simply shortened it. Arun's is pronounced the same as the English Aaron but spelt A-R-U-N, but for school he was Arun Rahman.'

'So, you're not who you said you were, but you've been this person you're not since you were seven?'

Kam turned to Jenny to see if she was teasing him, but no vestige of a smile flickered about her lips, and her eyes looked very stormy, golden glints darting like fire in the dim cave.

'Is that an excuse or an explanation?' she continued, her lovely lips, slightly swollen by their kisses, set in a thin, grim line.

'It's the beginning of an explanation,' Kam told her. 'My father changed our names because he feared we might be kidnapped if our real identity was known. Not that he'd have missed us, he was quite old by the time we were born and had little contact with us. But he'd worked his way through four wives in order to finally produce sons to ensure the succession, and for that reason he was wary.'

'Succession? Your father?' Jen pressed, and Kam understood the question.

'The hereditary ruler of our country—the one over the border—the sheikh who recently died.'

'So, let me get this straight,' Jen said, using the excuse of putting down her empty teacup to stand up then return and sit a little further apart from him. 'You're not Kam Rahman, but Kam something else—what comes after that?'

'Kamid Rahman al'Kawali,' Kam told her, wondering why his full name would matter.

Jen repeated the name in her head. It sounded nice. But the bud of hope had already withered on its stem. Even if he loved her—and there was not one single, solitary reason to think he might—he couldn't marry her. His marriage would be important to his country and his people, and apart from that, as the hereditary ruler he'd need to have children to carry on—sons doubtless. He'd already told her how important sons were...

Her heart ached with regrets she knew she shouldn't have, and certainly would have to hide.

Anger would help!

'And you couldn't tell me this right at the start? You had to be someone else. Was there a reason?'

Kam sighed.

'My father was ill for a long time, and things have deteriorated throughout the country. We are wealthy people, and always have been, even before oil was discovered here, having been successful traders from many centuries ago. And we've always prided ourselves on taking care of our own. So, imagine my surprise and disappointment when I discover there's a foreign aid organisation working in our country.'

'But you've been working here yourself, in the city, you said. Shouldn't you have known?'

Kam shook his head.

'I barely knew my father and, though ill, he kept control through his brothers and their sons. My father married four times, wanting sons but only having daughters until his last wife, my mother, produced male twins. Once we were born, that was enough for him. He went back to his favourite, his third wife. My mother was set up in her own house and we were raised by the women around her until he sent us to school in England. It could have been rebelling against him that made Arun and I decided to study medicine rather than go into businesses the family owned. That made relations between the two of us and our father even more strained so, although we worked here, it was as ordinary citizens, not as sheikhs or heirs to the old man.'

Jen thought of her own close family, without whose love and caring and support she'd never have recovered from the deaths of David and her unborn child. She remembered her childhood, filled with laughter and the confidence that came from knowing she was loved.

Her heart ached for the children the twins had been, for the childhood they'd never had...

'When our father died, both Arun and I would have preferred one of our uncles take over as ruler, but people came to us with disturbing reports that things were bad throughout the country. Someone told us of Aid for All, other reports were that government funds were being siphoned off to family members rather than being distributed evenly to the people. We didn't know if one uncle had gone bad or if all of them were in collusion, so how could we pass the succession to any of them?'

He paused, looking directly at Jenny, although the light was so dim she doubted he would see the despairing pity in her eyes.

'I came out here to see the work Aid for All is doing and to find out why we can't do it ourselves. After this camp I intended to travel through the other villages on or near the border so I could see for myself what was happening in the country, while Arun is checking what he can in the city.'

'Also incognito?'

Kam shook his head.

'He's too well known in the city—both of us are. And as well as that, the checking there needs influence—bankers and government officials—so his position is important for him to collect information. But out in the country people react differently to the ruler, particularly if they feel the family has been neglecting them. I wanted to see things for myself, and to work out ways to right genuine wrongs, not be told tales of woe by someone who might want nothing more than to make money out of an untenable situation.'

Jenny nodded, understanding all of this yet still feeling the deep hurt of betrayal. She had been suspicious of Kam and now knew her suspicions had been well founded.

So how much did it count that his reasons for deceit were good?

It didn't seem to help the pain she was feeling, or the devastation that had swamped her when she'd realised who Kam was, although the devastation, she knew, was to do with the shrivelling of the bud of hope that had sprouted from her love.

'Let's make some stew,' he suggested, standing up and offering his hand to help her up.

Jen didn't take it—couldn't—she was too confused, but as a child she'd played house as well as anyone, and a little make-believe might be what was needed to get them through until the sandstorm subsided and they could safely return to the camp.

She turned the wick on the lamp a little higher and set out the tins of food on the table.

'See, that's tinned corned beef, or that's what it looks like from the picture on the side,' she explained, putting the largest of the tins to one side. 'And there are tinned peas and tinned carrots and even tinned potatoes. An onion would be nice, and something to make gravy.'

Kam was studying the other tins, reading labels Jenny couldn't understand.

'This is soup, would that do?' he suggested. 'To make it into soup you add water so perhaps if we didn't add the water…'

He sounded so uncertain, this strong, confident man to whom uncertainty would surely be foreign, that Jenny longed to put her arms around him, to assure him that she understood why he had deceived her. But her own emotions were too raw to put on show, and touching him was likely to start the flaring heat between them, so she thanked him for finding the soup and set him to opening cans while she lit the little stove again.

With the cans opened, Kam then rummaged around at the back of the cave, muttering to himself about why the electricity wouldn't have been connected when the houses in the village all had it.

'I suppose because no one ever lived here permanently. It might have belonged to a family that only came in the summer,' Jenny suggested, chopping up the corned meat then putting it and the contents of the other tins into the saucepan and wondering what the resulting mess would taste like.

'Not too bad,' Kam announced when they finally sat down to eat. He'd found some flour and although Jen knew flour and water were the basic ingredients, she wasn't too sure about making flat-bread. But she'd tried and, though tough, the bread, cooked in a frying-pan that had been hanging on the back wall, didn't taste too bad.

'You don't suppose they've forgotten we're here,' she suggested, trying to make near to normal conversation in order to distract her thoughts from how good things had been between them during their first twenty-four hours in the cave.

'I don't think that's likely, but the wind has been so fierce no one would be venturing outside. It can blind a man, or push him over, so people shut themselves inside their tents or houses and wait it out. It won't last much longer. Already the keening of it is lessening, the sound less shrill, don't you think?'

Jen didn't answer, wanting to cry because the easy communion they'd enjoyed, the whispered endearments they'd shared as they'd made love, had been replaced by such banal conversation.

Conversation about the weather, of all things!

A touch would bridge the gap that had grown between them and have them back in bed within minutes, while conversation was widening the gap into a gully. But wasn't it better to let it widen—let it widen further from a gully to a gulch or even to a gorge?

She longed to touch him, but knew the parting would be harder if she did, and the parting was as inevitable as an ending to the storm.

'It was like a dream,' she said quietly. 'A very special dream, but like all dreams it had to come to an end.'

Kam didn't answer, couldn't...

He knew he'd lost her. He'd felt the shift in the closeness between them way back when she'd mentioned stew. Hard to believe that stew of all things—and a revolting stew at that— should have torn them apart.

Admittedly they had been due to be torn apart, or, if not torn, due to part. He had to move on to other places, she had work to finish in the camp. He had to sort out the succession and his country's problems and she lived for the adventure and fun and challenge of her work abroad.

But surely he could offer adventure, fun and challenge to her right here in his own country!

The thought startled him.

What was he thinking?

Marriage?

It certainly would have to be, because a woman like Jenny deserved no less.

There were precedents set in other Arab countries of a ruler marrying a foreigner, and in most cases that he knew of, the unions had been happy and successful.

'Would you marry me?' he asked, pushing away the rest of his stew and the almost inedible bread.

The idea had followed so closely on his previous thoughts he'd voiced the question without giving it much consideration. Until he saw the look of shock and disbelief on her face...

'What?' he demanded, not understanding either emotion.

'This all began back when I realised we didn't know each other, and we still don't—well, we don't know much about each other,' she grumbled. 'How can you possibly suggest marriage to someone you barely know, based solely on the grounds of good sex? And how could I even think about it when you've deceived me from the moment we met? What kind of a basis for marriage is that? Honestly, Kam, that was the most ridiculous suggestion I've ever heard. And who is the older of you two—you or your brother? It seems one of you will be the new ruler, so surely you'd need a wife from your own culture; surely that would be more acceptable to your people, especially if your father spent his last years alienating them.'

'I thought there had been more than good sex between us,' he replied, his chest hurting at the implications of that particular remark, while the other objections she'd brought up niggled at the edges of his mind with irritating insistence.

A shout from outside the cave broke into the strained atmosphere that had been worsening between them.

Kam went to the door to greet their guide and lead him inside.

He carried a covered cooking pot and the aroma rising from it suggested it was a tastier meal than the stew they'd just made.

'You will eat, then the woman will check the patient and I will take you back to the border. If the chief's wife is well and the baby, we will wait a few nights before we ask the doctor to come again.'

Kam agreed that this seemed very sensible but in a few nights he'd be gone, or should be. There was much to do and he'd already lingered too long.

But to let Jenny return here alone?

It was not only unthinkable but the thought caused him serious pain.

He took the cooking pot and set it on the table, assuring their guide they'd eat then go across to the women's tent.

The guide bowed to Jenny then departed while Kam translated what he'd said.

'If the mother's OK I could wait a week before returning,' Jen said, and Kam's stomach cramped a little harder. It *might* have been the canned soup stew, but Kam suspected it was fear for Jenny.

Fear?

Concern at least, but surely concern wasn't strong enough for stomach cramps.

So he was back to fear, but fear for a woman whom, as she had so succinctly pointed out, he barely knew?

Why?

Unless...

No, he wouldn't go there. Love had never been an issue in his life, maybe because he hadn't experienced it as a child. Not the warm, loving, laughing family type of love he'd read and heard about. He had friends, of course, but liking covered what he felt for them.

But love for other people, especially for a woman, wasn't something he'd thought much about, and he'd certainly never considered it could be a trigger for fear...

CHAPTER TEN

'I'LL get dressed and we'll go, shall we?' Jen suggested when they'd sat and looked at the stew pot for a while, and it had become obvious neither of them was going to eat.

She didn't wait for an answer, gathering up her clothes and taking them to the dark corner they had used as a bathroom, dressing as quickly as she could, pulling on her doctor persona with her clothes, hoping her mind would be strong enough to put all the side issues of Kam and sex and the end of love to one side while she examined the new mother and her baby.

He must have dressed while she had been dressing, for he now stood beside the hanging mats, ready to hold them for her as she left the cave.

But memories made her reluctant to just walk out, and her body ached with the knowledge that what they'd had was finished.

Over...

Done with...

Move on...

But her aching heart couldn't make the leap, and she could feel tears welling in her eyes and a lump in her throat.

'Do you think they'd mind if I took the cream?' she whispered, the lump in her throat making her voice so husky it was a wonder Kam heard her at all.

He cursed, long and fluently, and although she didn't understand the words, the crisp, almost bitter tone in which they had been uttered told her they weren't cries of delight. Then he took her in his arms and kissed her so savagely her knees went weak and only by clinging to his shoulders could she remain upright.

The magic worked again, her nipples peaking, breasts growing heavy, the newly sensitised place between her thighs tingling with anticipation. Her hands grasped him and held him tight and with the kiss she gave back to him she tried to tell him all she felt, tell him that she loved him and always would.

But who understood kisses?

And the one thing he shouldn't know was that she loved him…

They fell back on the bed, grappling with their clothes, not bothering to strip but finding each other and making love one final time, intense, passionate, mutually satisfying love.

Or was it sex?

Jen no longer knew or cared how Kam thought of it—to her it was an expression of her love, given freely and without remorse or regret. For this one brief time Kam was hers again…

Kam helped her fix her clothing, doing up her bra catch and buttoning her shirt. His fingers fumbled with the tasks.

Because he knew this was it?

This was the last time he would touch Jenny's clothes?

Touch Jenny?

Unless…

'Why wouldn't you marry me?' he asked when they were ready to leave, the jar of rose-scented cream clasped in Jenny's hands.

She smiled at him.

'There are probably as many reasons as there are grains of sand in this cave. First, there's your position in your country, and your duty to your country, and how your family would feel if you married a foreigner, and the fact that you don't love me and I wouldn't like a marriage without love, and so many more reasons that the baby in the women's tent would be a toddler before I finished listing them.'

Kam heard them all but took little notice, his mind having picked up on the 'you don't love me' reason, and halted there.

'How do you know I don't love you?' he demanded, and she had the hide to smile again.

'Do you?' she asked, and having deceived her once he couldn't do it again.

But he could dodge and weave a bit...

'I know so little about love,' he told her. 'I know I love my brother because we only had each other for a long time. We were ignored by our father, passed on to nurses and waiting women by our mother, then sent to boarding school in a cold, hard, foreign country from the age of seven. We clung to each other, and grew to think and act as one, facing life and all its challenges together, and probably, at the same time, shutting out friends we might have had, for a while at least.'

'But you do have friends?' Jen pressed, and he nodded.

'Good friends, and each of us have different sets of friends, but I'd say liking is what I feel for them, not love.'

'And women? Surely at some stage of your life there's been a woman who set your pulses racing, and made your chest hurt when you were apart, and made your heart do a little flip when you saw her again after being parted?'

Kam tried to think.

'Pulse racing, yes, but that's attraction and desire. I couldn't call what I've ever felt for a woman love.'

Jen stood on tiptoe to kiss him gently on the lips.

'Then I feel sorry for you, Kam, although love hurts and losing a loved one is probably the most painful, agonising, gut-wrenching, heart-slamming hurt of all. But without it in our lives there's an emptiness, a void, a space we try to fill with other things, like challenge and adventure and fun.'

There was a pause and then she added, 'Which works for a time, of course.'

She ducked out of the cave before he could answer and, afraid she might get lost, he followed.

What had she been saying?

What had that final remark meant?

That challenge, adventure and fun were no longer enough?

That she'd found love again?

That she loved him?

He reached out a hand to stop her before she walked into the women's tent, but it was too late. She'd slipped off her sandals at the entrance and was already greeting the women inside.

Kam trudged around the tent to the place where he was used to waiting, ready to translate anything too medical or female oriented for the chief to tackle. But the chief wasn't there.

'What's happening?' Kam asked the guide who waited in the chief's place.

'The chief is at a meeting. If there is any problem with his wife or child I am to get him, but if not, he is not to be interrupted. It seems the arrival of his son has made him reconsider his claims on this territory. They are holding peace talks in the tent, but he has a message for the woman doctor. If the war is settled, will her organisation test his people for TB as she is doing for the refugees? It would be bad for them to come back if some people here still have the disease.'

'I can guarantee a testing and treatment programme for you—tell him that,' Kam said, then, in case the guide might be suspicious of his ability to make such a promise, he added, 'I work for the same organisation.' That was true. A donation to Aid for All had ensured he could move around his country under their banner. 'But I am in a higher position.'

The guide and the chief would accept this happily, their own customs suggesting a man would always be in a higher position than a woman.

Jenny's voice stopped the conversation. She was asking Kam to tell the woman that all was well, her wound was healing beautifully, the baby doing well, and they wouldn't need to come back for a few days, when Jenny would take out the stitches.

'Could you also tell the midwife what a great job she has done in looking after the pair, and tell her that although we would love to work out a way to teach her about Caesareans, the difficulty would be the anaesthetic and also if there were complications during or after the operation, unexpected haemorrhage, for instance. Perhaps you could tell her that your country is setting up a new air medical service, with doctors from the hospitals in the city working by roster to take emergency trips out to the far reaches of the country, and neighbouring countries as well.'

Confused though he'd been feeling, especially as far as Jenny was concerned, Kam had to smile. Talk about getting her pound of flesh! Now she knew who he was and how fervently he and Arun wished to make amends to their countrymen, she'd no doubt be coming up with more schemes like that, although an air medical service *was* a good idea. It was easy enough to build runways in the desert.

Somewhat reassured by the idea that peace talks were under way and Jenny's return in a few days might be all the safer because of that, Kam made the arrangements, though determined, when he radioed Arun on his return to the camp, to ask him to send someone out who could act as interpreter but also guard her safety.

Someone with enough authority to see that she remained safe while in the rebel camp.

He couldn't think offhand of anyone he'd trust that far and the thought worried him, but Jenny was speaking again, saying she was finished and would he please say goodbye to the women for her.

'There are a couple more pregnant women here,' she told him when she met him at the door of the tent minutes later. 'So you might need that aerial medical service sooner than you think, although I'll be here for another month or so myself. Could you tell them that and tell them if they want me to come to see them, or want to come across to the clinic, I'd be only too happy to check on them?'

'You can't cross back and forth across the border,' Kam told her, the irrational anger he felt at her putting herself in danger seizing him again. 'Have you forgotten the danger? The way we were treated on our first visit?'

'Ah, but now we're friends,' Jen told him. 'The chief is a question mark, but his wife, the midwife and the other women have begun to trust me, and trust leads to friendship. I can't believe they have no say in the running of their lives and no influence with their menfolk. Their friendship will protect me.'

'You are too trusting for your own good,' Kam snapped at

her. 'I don't want you coming back and forth over the border, no matter how many women are pregnant.'

'Don't you, now?' she snapped right back. 'And I should care because?'

'Because I—'

He heard the words he was about to utter in a kind of practice in his head and caught them just in time, then as it dawned on him they were the stark, honest truth, he said them anyway.

'Because I love you,' he said, and though his heart was hammering with the emotion of the declaration and his body shivering with reaction, he still took in the look of shock imprinted on her lovely face.

'Oh, but, Kam, you can't,' she wailed, desperation seeding the words with misery.

'Why can't I?' he demanded, angered now he'd made his declaration and she'd deflected it. For answer she studied him in silence for a moment then she took his face between the palms of her hands and looked into his eyes.

'Because your country means so much to you, more even than I think you realise. And to do your duty to it, you must marry and have children.'

Then, oblivious of the people around them, she reached up and kissed him on the lips.

'I can't have children,' she whispered against his lips, then with a quick, final hug she released him.

But he was not ready to let go.

'Can't? The accident? You know for sure?'

'Ninety per cent sure,' she said gently, and turned to greet their guide, who'd come to take them back to the border.

Kam forced his numbed mind to work enough to give orders to his legs, moving like a robot behind the pair. Once beyond the light at the entrance to the women's tent, the dust still lingering in the air blocked out any moonlight or starlight, so they followed closely in the wake of the guide, their feet shuffling through drifts of sand and stumbling over piles of it in unexpected places.

Kam held the door for Jenny as she climbed into the car, but knew he couldn't talk to her about this until they were alone.

Which didn't stop him pondering the problem.

She'd lost a baby in the accident—what other damage might have been caused?

He felt his heart squeeze with pain at the thought—remembering Jenny with Rosana, remembering the love she felt for the little boys, her concern for Hamid. Jenny giving her love to other people's children...

The guide dropped them back at the border and they crossed into the camp, and even in the dim night light they could see the sand piled against the tents, in some places women sweeping at it, trying to move it away.

'It could make the whole camp disappear if it blew long enough,' Jenny murmured as they looked around.

Just like that—normal conversation. Love, attraction, sex, whatever it had been put behind them—as far as she was concerned.

But what about *him*? He had all the symptoms she'd mentioned. The racing pulse, the hurting chest and the little flip of his heart when he'd seen her putting on her sandals at the women's tent, although their time apart had only been a matter of minutes...

He wanted to talk about it, but she was pointing out the way the sand had built up against his vehicle and wondering if he'd be able to get it out.

'You'll be leaving, won't you?' Jen said, knowing he had a job to finish, hoping the sooner he left, the sooner her heart would start to heal.

Hoping the sooner he left, the less chance there was of revealing her feelings for him.

'Tomorrow—I should go tomorrow,' he told her, moving closer so she knew it wasn't a departure time he wanted to talk about, but personal things.

'That's for the best,' she told him, then turned towards him, looking up at him in the dim light, the moon nothing more than a suggestion in the still dusty air. 'It was wonderful, Kam, and I'll never forget what we had. Fun, challenge and adventure, all my desires rolled into one.'

'*All* your desires?'

'All I've wished for since David's death,' she said, which was the truth as far as it went, but a truth that had changed when she'd met Kam.

He grasped her shoulders and gave her a little shake.

'Not love? Have you banned love from your life because you lost one man you loved—because you suffered pain? Would you deny yourself the pleasure of it once again, just to avoid hurt? You talk to me of how empty my life must have been to have not loved, yet you've shut off *your* heart behind barriers, travelling the world, helping others, moving on, in case you become too attached to a particular place or person and in losing it or him or her, you'd hurt again. I thought you brave, courageous, but you're not— you're a coward, too afraid of the consequences to grasp at happiness.'

'I can't, Kam,' she said, keeping her voice steady with an effort. Knowing she couldn't say another word without breaking down, she walked into the big tent that was her home, clutching her arms across her chest to still her hammering, hurting heart.

Jen cradled Rosana in her arms as she watched the car approach, hoping as always it would stop before the tents so the dust that trailed it would not go into the clinic. Was it because she held Rosana again this morning that she remembered Kam's arrival? The child weighed more now and chattered cheerfully, her life with the boys as guardians obviously suiting her.

And was she, Jen, thinking of Rosana to stop herself thinking of Kam, arriving like this in a far less shiny car only a little over a week ago?

She wasn't going to answer that, mainly because thinking of Kam was a full-time occupation. They didn't interfere with her work, but the memories were always there in the back of her mind, memories of warmth and laughter and his gentle touch along her scars.

You couldn't see the new scars…

The dust settled and she realised this was a very different vehicle, splendidly large and shiny beneath its patina of dust. A figure emerged from the far side, a figure in a flowing white gown, hands upraised to secure the shiny black double braid that held his scarf in place.

Jen couldn't help but stare. This was an image from fairy stories and fancy magazines, the tall, strong desert warrior in his snowy robes—his stance, his presence casting awe on all who saw him.

She smiled at the thought for the little boys, who'd come running when they'd heard the car, now stood back, heads bowing, something akin to fear on their faces. Then the figure knelt and held out his hands and the boys moved closer, smiling now, shyly touching his robes.

Kam!

Heart thudding, Jen held Rosana closer, the urge to flee tingling in her legs.

But she wouldn't run away.

She and Kam were finished, they both understood that. Besides, another man had now emerged from the vehicle, a tall, tanned man who came closer, smiling at Jen, holding out his hand, his green eyes...

Had she been mistaken about the first man?

Had she got over Kam so quickly her heart didn't thud and her stomach didn't cramp and her breathing didn't hitch in her throat when he approached?

'You know I'm not him, don't you?' the man said.

Jenny whispered, 'Arun?'

He nodded but looked a little put out.

'I thought as you'd never seen him in his local gear you might not have known it was him. So why didn't you, Dr Jenny Stapleton? We're identical. Everyone mistakes us.'

Jen smiled at him.

'You didn't make my heart beat faster,' she admitted, feeling a weight lift off her shoulders as she spoke, knowing he would understand it as a declaration of her love. 'But if you tell Kam I said that, I'll deny it.'

She glanced across to where the man who did make her heart beat faster had last been, but he'd disappeared, although a few of the boys were still there by the car.

'I won't tell Kam but I did suspect you must love him. From all I've heard—and, believe me, I've heard plenty—I suspected you might feel the same way about him as he feels about you. So why, Jenny Stapleton, won't you marry him?'

Rosana was wriggling in her arms and the man who wasn't Kam reached out and took her, murmuring gentle words to the child, making her clap her hands and giggle with delight.

'He didn't tell you?

The little boys—the blood brothers—appeared and took Rosana, and Arun followed Jen into the tent.

The women in there fell about in their eagerness to serve him, and watching Arun charm them Jen was glad it was Kam she loved, not him. Charm came less easily to Kam, he used respect in all his dealings and earned it in return.

She watched as Arun was served his coffee, and little sweetmeats and cakes were offered on a tray, then as the women withdrew, Jen raised her coffee-cup towards him.

'Did you wear the full outfit today to impress the locals?'

'Ouch!' he said, and tried to look hurt, although his green eyes glinted with humour and she couldn't help but like him.

'Actually, it's the full outfit because I'm on official business. We both are. We have an engineer with us and he's going to check out the site for the best place to sink a well, then Kam and I are meeting with the chief across the border to discuss a trans-border arrangement for an aerial medical service and to work out a timetable for the refugees to return to their village.'

He paused, smiling at Jenny.

'I understand you had not a little to do with the medical service suggestion.'

Jen shook her head, unable to believe it might be happening so quickly.

'I didn't think he'd do anything about it—not right away

when he, and you, I suppose, have so many other pressing problems.'

Arun smiled again.

'I think any suggestion you made would be acted on immediately, Jenny. And, anyway, the other pressing problems have become less pressing. Kam has agreed to take over the succession, our uncles have stepped down from their positions and government workers from within the various departments will take over their—Jenny! What's wrong?'

She managed to put down her cup before the wooziness made her spill the contents, and she reached out for the ground to stop herself from fainting head first into the plate of cakes. Arun came swiftly to her side and steadied her, his strong arms holding her until the faintness passed.

'I'm all right,' she managed, but the words that had caused her faintness—*Kam has agreed to take over the succession*—echoed in her head, ripping out the last faint threads of hope she'd stupidly been clinging to.

'It was— I…'

No words would come, for nothing could explain the emptiness inside her.

'Tell me,' Arun said, and suddenly Jenny knew that all she felt could no longer be contained within her pounding head, or hidden in her hurting heart.

'Tell you what? That I love Kam? That's easy to tell, Arun, because I do. With all my heart and soul and being. I never expected to feel love like that again then, bang, love suddenly slammed into me like a train. But it was Kam Rahman that I loved and I even began to hope he might love me back—it was like a miracle. Then he wasn't Kam Rahman but had other names tacked on which made him heir to the throne of a sheikhdom, and that made everything impossible.'

She stopped, already having said more than she should have, worrying about Arun repeating it to Kam.

But Kam must surely know she loved him even if she hadn't said it...

'Go on,' Arun said, and she looked at him, frowning, wondering what more there was to say.

'Why impossible?' he prompted. 'And don't tell me it's because you're a foreigner, because foreigners have been marrying into our family for centuries—where did you think Kam's and my green eyes came from?'

'It wasn't just the foreigner thing,' Jen admitted, sensing Arun wasn't going to let it go and wanting to talk about it anyway. 'I was eight months pregnant when we had the accident that killed my husband. I lost the baby as well and the damage caused at the time means I can't have children.'

She tried a smile she knew was a bit wobbly on her lips.

'A foreigner might have been OK, but a foreigner who can't produce heirs? That would be impossible—I couldn't do it to him. Marrying Kam when he already has so many problems to sort out, and when he, and you, are trying so desperately to pull Zaheer together after years of neglect. No, he needs a wife of the people, someone who understands what has to be done and can help and support him—someone who speaks the language, for a start!'

She paused, then added bleakly, 'But most of all he needs someone who can give him sons!'

She shook her head and hoped the tears she knew were welling in her eyes didn't overflow and go streaming down her cheeks, but when Arun put his arms around her and drew her close against his body, so she felt it could be Kam who was holding her one last time, she couldn't hold them back.

But indulgence in such weakness couldn't be allowed to go on, so she pulled away within a minute, straightening up, sniffing back the tears, swallowing the sad lump in her throat and asking him if he'd like to see the camp or the testing programme before they met the guide at the border in an hour.

'I'd rather talk to you,' Arun told her, but she shook her head.

'I've already talked far too much,' she said. '*Far* too much! I'll get over Kam and he—if he really loves me—will get over me, especially as he has to juggle his new role as ruler and his medical work, and life will go on for both of us. I've been told of an AIDS testing programme in Africa I can join when I finish here. It's in place I've never been.'

'Adventure, challenge, fun!' Arun said, and Jen began to wonder just how much information brothers—twins—might share. Not all of it, she hoped…

'That's right,' she said. 'It's not for everyone, but it suits me.'

'Suits you to run away.'

Arun spoke so sternly Jen stared at him.

'I'm not running away,' she said. 'I'm moving on, as I always intended to.'

'You *are* running away. You're running away from love because it hurt you once before. You're using the excuse of being a foreigner and not being able to have a child, but basically it's because you're a coward.'

'You can't say that!' Jenny snapped, really annoyed with the man now. 'You don't even know me!'

'No, and I don't know that I want to, because I would have thought the woman Kam finally fell in love with had more guts.'

'Guts?' Jen echoed weakly, still annoyed but wondering what on earth Arun was getting at.

'The guts to fight for him—to fight for happiness for both of you. So what if you can't have children? In another fifty years—even thirty—inherited positions could well be a thing of the past.'

Jenny stared at Arun. Was he right? Was she gutless?

No! If Arun was right and Kam truly loved her, wouldn't he be here? Wouldn't she be talking to him rather than Arun? Wouldn't he have wanted, on arrival, to speak to her, touch her, at least to hold her hand?

The fact that he was walking through the camp in search of a site for a well told her all she needed to know—duty came first for him and, sadly, that was how it should be.

The little boys arrived to tell them the guide was waiting, and Jen was relieved to set aside her doubts and follow her little friends towards the border. She introduced Arun to the guide and saw the proud man bow his head towards Arun, then open the car door for him. Jen opened the back door for herself, recognising her place in the local scheme of things— one of relative unimportance.

At the village over the border Arun translated ably, and Jen removed the stitches and pronounced her patient well, the baby beautiful, and all the pregnant women in sound health. Arun spoke again, but in his own language, and soon the women clustered around Jenny, leading her to a mat where tea and coffee were laid out, and plates laden with dates and other fruit and sweets set in the middle.

'You will eat and enjoy the women's company,' a deep voice announced, and Jenny turned to see the chief in the doorway, Arun just beyond him. Another order was issued and the midwife took the baby to the chief who presented him proudly to Arun.

It seemed for ever before she heard male voices approaching the women's tent and the chief appeared once again in the doorway.

'You are ready to return?'

Jenny nodded, getting to her feet, thanking the women who had entertained and fed her, using the few words of Arabic she knew and hoping they were the right words. Then she walked to the doorway of the tent where the men waited just beyond the entrance, the chief in his usual black robe, Arun contrasting in his white. She bent to fasten a sandal, wobbling slightly as she did so. A strong hand reached out to steady her, and awareness shot like an arc of electricity right through her body.

'Kam?' she whispered, turning towards the man in the white gown who now held her steady.

He *had* come!

The white-clad figure nodded, his green eyes looking deep into hers.

'Did you think I'd take your no and walk away?' he said. 'How could I when you'd taught me what love was like? I know you believe you'd do my position harm by marrying me, but have you thought what harm you'd do my heart? Do you know what the only valid reason for not marrying me would be? That you didn't love me.'

He turned her so he could study her face, and Jen realised the chief had moved away and they were alone.

'Can you tell me that? Look me in the eyes and say it? I don't think you can, Jenny, because I think you love me as much as I love you, and do you know how much that is? As boundless as the desert, that's my love, as strong as the storm that brought us such delights, as incalculable as the number of grains of sand on which we stand. Do you think I would prefer a wife I didn't love, or that I would not marry you because you couldn't produce an heir? I have a brother who can do that, and cousins should Arun not marry. It is not an issue, Jenny, when set against the love I feel for you.'

He paused, then bent his head and kissed her thoroughly, withdrawing only far enough to question her again.

'*Now* tell me you don't love me,' he whispered, and Jen stared at him in confusion.

'I *do* love you,' she managed, 'but it still seems wrong.'

'How could it be wrong if love lies between us, Jenny? Is it not said that love will find a way? Love will find our way, and light our path, and lead us wherever life is meant to take us. So marry me and share the journey, share the joy that love will bring us, without thoughts of other things or regrets for what might have been. Just love, Jen, and you and me.'

Jenny snuggled closer to him.

'You and me and however many thousands of people you rule over,' she teased.

'Well, yes, there's them, and my family, and your family— but at the heart of it all is us.'

'Us,' Jen echoed, and felt all the turmoil she'd been feeling in her heart and head ease into happiness. 'Us,' she whispered again, reaching up to kiss Kam on the lips.

THE MARRIAGE BARGAIN

Bid for, bargained for, bound forever!

A merciless Spaniard, a British billionaire,
an arrogant businessman and a ruthless tycoon:
these men have one thing in common—they're all
in the bidding for a bride!

There's only one answer to their proposals they'll
accept—and they will do whatever it takes to
claim a willing wife....

**Look for all the exciting stories,
available in June:**

The Millionaire's Chosen Bride #57
by SUSANNE JAMES

His Bid for a Bride #58
by CAROLE MORTIMER

The Spaniard's Marriage Bargain #59
by ABBY GREEN

Ruthless Husband, Convenient Wife #60
by MADELEINE KER

HARLEQUIN *Presents*

NIGHTS *of* PASSION

One night is never enough!

These guys know what they want
and how they're going to get it!

PLEASURED BY THE SECRET MILLIONAIRE
by Natalie Anderson

Rhys Maitland has gone incognito—he's sick of
women wanting him only for his looks and money!
He wants more than one night with passionate
Sienna, but she has her own secrets....

Book #2834

Available June 2009

Catch all these hot stories where sparky romance
and sizzling passion are guaranteed!

www.eHarlequin.com   HP12834

REQUEST YOUR FREE BOOKS!

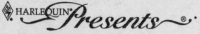

2 FREE NOVELS PLUS 2 FREE GIFTS!

YES! Please send me 2 FREE Harlequin Presents® novels and my 2 FREE gifts (gifts are worth about $10). After receiving them, if I don't wish to receive any more books, I can return the shipping statement marked "cancel". If I don't cancel, I will receive 6 brand-new novels every month and be billed just $4.05 per book in the U.S. or $4.74 per book in Canada. That's a savings of close to 15% off the cover price! It's quite a bargain! Shipping and handling is just 50¢ per book*. I understand that accepting the 2 free books and gifts places me under no obligation to buy anything. I can always return a shipment and cancel at any time. Even if I never buy another book, the two free books and gifts are mine to keep forever.

106 HDN EYRQ 306 HDN EYR2

Name	(PLEASE PRINT)	
Address		Apt. #
City	State/Prov.	Zip/Postal Code

Signature (if under 18, a parent or guardian must sign)

Mail to the **Harlequin Reader Service:**
IN U.S.A.: P.O. Box 1867, Buffalo, NY 14240-1867
IN CANADA: P.O. Box 609, Fort Erie, Ontario L2A 5X3

Not valid to current subscribers of Harlequin Presents books.

Are you a current subscriber of Harlequin Presents books and want to receive the larger-print edition? Call 1-800-873-8635 today!

* Terms and prices subject to change without notice. Prices do not include applicable taxes. Sales tax applicable in N.Y. Canadian residents will be charged applicable provincial taxes and GST. Offer not valid in Quebec. This offer is limited to one order per household. All orders subject to approval. Credit or debit balances in a customer's account(s) may be offset by any other outstanding balance owed by or to the customer. Please allow 4 to 6 weeks for delivery. Offer available while quantities last.

Your Privacy: Harlequin Books is committed to protecting your privacy. Our Privacy Policy is available online at www.eHarlequin.com or upon request from the Reader Service. From time to time we make our lists of customers available to reputable third parties who may have a product or service of interest to you. If you would prefer we not share your name and address, please check here. ☐

HP09R

HARLEQUIN *Presents*

*Sicilian by name...scandalous,
scorching and seductive by nature!*

THE SICILIAN'S
BABY BARGAIN
by **Penny Jordan**

Falcon Leopardi will claim his late half brother's
child from vulnerable Annie—but duty means he
must also protect her. The women of his sultry island
will mourn: Falcon is taking a wife!

Book #2827

Available June 2009

Look out for more fabulous stories
from Penny Jordan, coming soon
in Harlequin Presents!